I0579101

Call

of the

Dragon

Marked by the Dragon Book 3

RICHARD FIERCE

Dragonfire Press

Copyright © 2021 Richard Fierce

All rights reserved. All events portrayed in this book are fictitious, and any resemblance to real people or events is purely coincidental. All rights reserved, including the right to reproduce this book or portions thereof in any form without the express permission of the publisher.

Cover design by germancreative.

Cover art by Rosauro Ugang

ISBN: 978-1-947329-84-3

CONTENTS

MAP

1

When Mina arrived at the underground city that Copper called home, the first thing she noticed was the heat. It was located deep within The Long Sands, and she was drenched in sweat by the time they landed. A few dragons flew overhead, wheeling around in lazy circles.

What are they doing?

They are scouts, Copper replied. *They keep watch for sand wyrms.*

She thought about the one she had seen before and shivered at the memory.

You are safe here. Even if one got past the scouts, it would face an army of us.

What if more than one came?

They are not intelligent enough to band together.

His answer gave her some relief. That was one thing she didn't have to worry about. She slid off Copper's back and groaned. Her rear end was sore, as were her back and legs, and her fingers were cramped. She stretched them by making fists and releasing them, trying to work the stiffness out.

Many of the dragons here have not seen a human in centuries. I expect you'll not receive a warm welcome.

Will they try to hurt me?

No. And if they did, I would not allow it. You are bonded to me, and it is my duty to protect you.

Even from your own kind?

Yes.

Mina hoped for both their sakes that it wouldn't come to that.

Follow me, Copper said. *You can rest in my chamber.*

The dragon walked down into the sloped cave-like entrance, and Mina trailed behind him. Thick glass formed the walls and ceiling, and unnatural light flickered within it, illuminating their way as they lost the sunlight behind them.

Where did all this glass come from? Mina asked.

We made it.

With magic?

Copper laughed at the question. *With our flames. Sand turns to glass under extreme heat.*

Truly? I didn't know that. She paused. *Why did you use glass?*

Sand on its own is weak. We wouldn't be able to tunnel through it without something to keep it from collapsing. We dragons like to see our reflections, so glass was the logical choice.

Mina stared at the wall to her right and watched their likenesses drifting along beside them. Lord

Klodian had ornate mirrors and windows, but they were nothing in comparison. The deeper they traveled, the cooler the air became. By the time they reached Copper's chamber, she was no longer sweating.

Inside, an enormous pool with crystal clear water drew her attention. She wanted nothing more than to bathe in it and wash the grime from her body.

Go ahead, Copper bade. *I must go and speak with the elders.*

You want me to stay here, alone?

You'll be fine so long as you don't venture out of my chamber. Until certain things are decided, you must stay in here.

That sounded like she was a prisoner, and Mina didn't like it. What could she do, though? She was a defenseless human surrounded by dragons.

How long will you be gone? she asked.

Not long. Wash yourself, and when I return, I will teach you some things that you will need to know before you go before the elders.

What kind of things?

Don't worry about that now. Go.

Mina walked to the edge of the water and looked over her shoulder, glimpsing Copper's tail as it swished out of view. She wondered how she was safe when the chamber had no door, but she pushed the thought away. If Copper said he would protect her, then she had to believe him. She stripped out of her clothes and tossed them into the pool, then stepped into the water.

The temperature was cool, but not cold. She submerged herself to her neck and sighed, feeling relaxed. Her clothes floated nearby, and she grabbed them and rung them out, setting them on the edge of the pool to dry. After Mina had washed the sweat and filth from her body, she left the pool and drip-dried.

There was nothing to warm her clothes with, and they were still damp when Copper returned. Mina hid from his view by holding the wet clothes against her body. He snorted in response.

I care nothing for your nakedness.

It feels weird letting anyone see me, whether we are the same species or not.

I forgot how sensitive humans were. It's no wonder that your lifespans are so short.

Mina rolled her eyes. *I'm not sensitive. I'm just ...*

Self-conscious? Copper asked.

Yes.

He snorted again.

Can you dry my clothes?

Sure. Set them on the ground.

Mina hesitantly did so, then quickly stood up and tried awkwardly to cover herself with her arms.

Copper ignored her and opened his mouth, setting the clothes on fire with a gust of his flaming breath. Mina's eyes widened in shock.

Why did you do that?

You don't need those rags anymore. You are dragon-bonded, and so you shall dress appropriately. Your new chamber is beside mine. Do you see the cleft there?

Mina followed his gaze to a spot in the glass wall that was darker than the rest.

That is a passage that connects our chambers. When we first built this place, we added rooms for our bonded. We had hoped that the spell the elders cast would eventually fade and that we would bond with humans again. That never happened, but we kept the rooms anyway. This is your new home if you so choose.

What of the elders? Mina asked. *Won't they have a problem with me being here?*

That remains to be seen, Copper replied. *They have agreed to hear your petition, so get dressed. The clothes in there should fit you, but let me know if they do not. Once you are ready, I will teach you about the Enclave.*

The Enclave?

Go, Copper bade. *We have little time before the elders call upon you.*

Mina nodded and made an embarrassing dash to the passage. It was only about six feet in length, and then she found herself in more familiar surroundings. The room was decorated with human decor. There was a bed and a wardrobe, as well as a large rug and a manakin with a suit of leather armor.

She wandered over to the wardrobe and opened the double doors. Black pants and a blue shirt caught her eye, and she quickly put them on. Casting a glance at herself in the mirror, she saw that she looked different somehow. Perhaps it was an illusion, or perhaps she only thought she looked different.

Are you ready yet? Copper asked.

Yes.

Mina looked at the manakin and wondered if she would end up wearing the armor. She was not a warrior, but that didn't mean she couldn't become one.

Can you teach me to fight? she asked.

Perhaps. If you sway the elders, your potential is limitless.

Mina's eyes lingered on the armor a moment longer, then she went back into Copper's room. She was going to do whatever it took to impress the elders.

2

There was nothing.

He was nothing, just an ethereal thought floating amid the unknown. Something indistinct floated near him. As he stared at it, it became clearer, more defined. It was five letters arranged in a specific pattern.

Caden.

His name, perhaps? Yes, there was something about it that rang true within his spirit. He tried to reach for it, but he had no hands or arms. A voice spoke the name, his name, and it echoed all around him.

Come to me.

Caden's eyes snapped open and he gasped in a deep breath. He laid there, confused. What had happened? Where had he been? The memory was already vague, and soon it was gone completely. He was staring up at the sky, the blue vastness of it more striking than he remembered.

Rise, and come to me.

The voice sounded familiar to him, and yet he couldn't place it. A strange feeling, to be sure. Caden sat up and looked around. A blackened field stretched in all directions. He touched the black stuff with his fingers and inspected them.

Ash.

Slowly, the events came back to him. He'd been murdered. Or at least, they had *tried* to murder him. Strangely, he was still alive. Another mystery. He stood on shaky legs and wondered how long he'd been out. The smoke he'd breathed in must have caused him to lose consciousness. Not far away, he saw the bodies of horses and their riders. He didn't have to see them up close to know they were Runesmen. Lord D'Lance's cruelty and malice knew no bounds.

He had survived, which meant that he could take the knowledge of what he'd learned to Lord Culver. Once the High Prince learned of Lord D'Lance's treachery, there would be hell to pay. Caden ran his tongue across his cracked lips. He needed water and food, in that order. Shelter too, but that could wait. He'd slept under the stars plenty of times. As he turned to the east, he felt something pulling at him.

Go north.

It was that voice again. Caden turned to the north and stared ahead. If he went that way, it would mean going back into Lord D'Lance's dominion. He knew he should probably go east to Lord Culver, but the voice that called to him was so very strong. His curiosity was too much, and he walked across the field, following the pull he felt.

He walked for hours, crossing over rivers and open fields, and navigating through darker landscapes that were bereft of life. The voice guided him the entire way. His clothes became dirty, his feet blistered, yet he pushed himself onward until he reached the base of a jagged mountain. Clouds had gathered overhead, signaling rain. Lightning flashed, and thunder rumbled a moment later. He was close now. The source of the voice was up there somewhere.

Caden began climbing the mountain.

At first, it was easy. Then the rain started, pattering softly here and there until it became a downpour, forcing him to scramble on all fours up the treacherous terrain. The water made it more perilous. The voice was stronger here, filled with power, and he focused on it, ignoring the pain in his muscles.

His clothes became soaked and stuck to his skin, annoying and awkward. Caden didn't relent. He continued up the face of the mountain until he reached a plateau. As he pulled himself onto it, he saw the shadowy ingress of a cave. Crumbling pillars engraved with symbols lined the entrance, standing guard silently.

Glancing behind him, Caden realized just how far he'd come. The base of the mountain was lost far below, hidden by the clouds and the rain. The air was thinner up here, and it was colder. He shivered and turned his gaze back to the entrance, staring into the inky blackness.

Enter, the voice bade.

How could he refuse? He'd come this far. Inexorably, his feet took him into the shadows. Once he passed between the pillars, the darkness took his sight and it forced him to feel along the wall with his hands. The stones were smooth, and Caden somehow knew this wasn't a natural cave at all, but a tunnel built by mortal hands.

He followed it blindly for so long that he thought he would be forever lost, but the voice strengthened his resolve. Ahead, he saw a faint green light. It was coming from the moss that had grown along the walls and across the ceiling. The glow illuminated the way, and he walked with confidence.

The tunnel opened up into a large circular chamber. The remains of what Caden assumed was an old temple were scattered around the room. He had a vague feeling that he'd seen this place before, but he knew that wasn't possible. He had never been to this mountain before, never knew of its existence until the voice had called him there.

Still, it *felt* familiar to him somehow. Perhaps he'd dreamt of it.

Yes, Caden thought. *I've been here in my dreams.*

He made his way closer to the ruined structure and stopped when something in the shadows moved. Fear crept into the back of his mind, and he grabbed the hilt of his sword. He couldn't die here, not like this. Alone. Forgotten. The voice soothed those fears.

Come inside.

Caden hesitated for only a moment, then he stepped inside the open doorway. Judging by the hinges on the frame, it was obvious there had once been a door attached. Inside, there was an altar with a bowl that rested atop it. From the looks of things, a fire had ravaged the place. The floor was covered in a thick layer of gray ash, and the crumbling walls were black with soot.

Behind the altar was a tall chair that reminded him of a throne. And behind the throne, he caught sight of two glowing eyes. Caden's heart raced in his chest, but as the seconds slipped by and nothing happened, he calmed himself. There was nothing to fear. The voice would protect him, just as it had on his journey here.

Before, there had only been the voice in his mind, but now, there was a presence. It loomed in the shadows behind the throne.

"Who are you?" Caden asked. He kept his hand on the hilt of his blade.

You don't recognize me?

"No."

Mankind has forgotten me, the voice mused. *I was worshipped by men long ago. One goddess among many. I was here in the beginning. I owned the skies before men walked the earth, before their greed drove them to hurt me. You wouldn't hurt me, would you?*

Caden wondered why anyone would hurt her. She offered comfort and peace, provided protection where nothing else could. He had an epiphany, then. It was she who had kept him from the brink of death. Lord D'Lance had betrayed him, but she had saved him.

"I will never hurt you," Caden vowed.

That is good. We must have trust, you and I.

The eyes behind the throne blinked lazily.

I grow weary of being forced here. There is something you must do for me.

"What is it?" He would do anything for her.

The man who imprisoned me is the one you call Lord D'Lance. He is a wicked man, a foe to all of my kind. There is a room in his castle where he performs his dark deeds. Do you know of it?

"I'm afraid not," Caden replied. "But I will find it."

I trust you will. Inside the room, there should be a gemstone. It was created by Lord D'Lance to hurt me and keep me here in these ruins. Even now, its power sears my very being. I need you to destroy it.

"I will destroy it," Caden swore, removing his hand from the hilt and placing it on his chest. "And I will kill Lord D'Lance."

No! The voice hissed. *His death will come at my claws when I am ready.*

"You can trust me. I will spare him for you."

He will try to stop you. He will say many things to dissuade you from this course. You must not believe them.

"I will not believe his lies," Caden said.

The glowing eyes twinkled with satisfaction.

Once you have the stone, I will tell you how to destroy it. It will not be easy, but the cost will be worth it. You will be my general, and I will gather many to our cause. You will lead them all.

"I am not worthy."

I will make you worthy.

Caden could feel her power pulsing, expanding throughout the chamber. Ripples in the air drifted toward him and he held out his hand to touch them. Electricity touched his fingertips, filtering through his body. Caden could feel the raw power coursing through him, and it was exhilarating.

A tremor shook the mountain. Loose rocks clattered on the ground, joining the chittering of bats and other subterranean creatures that awoke from the disturbance. The voice spoke a single word.

Go.

3

Tell me again.

Mina forced her eyes closed and tried to be patient. Copper was trying to get her to memorize an abundance of facts about the elders and dragons, but it was just too much information for her to take in all at once.

There are seven elders that rule the desert, and all of them are from the metallic colors.

Good. Keep going.

Every 100 years, they switch places with another set of elders. They do this for many reasons, but mainly to prevent keeping the brethren stuck in their ways. Every group of elders leads differently. They are all to be respected because they are both wise and powerful.

Copper stared at her with slitted eyes and nodded his head. *When you are standing before the Enclave, what must you remember?*

That I should not speak out of turn, Mina replied.

And?

Mina huffed in a breath. *And I should address the elders as Tiarna.*

I think you are ready.

I don't feel ready.

Movement near the cave entrance caught Mina's attention. A silver dragon looked at Copper and bowed his head, then left.

We're out of time, Copper said. *The elders have summoned us.*

You'll be there with me?

Yes, but I will remain silent. The petition is yours, so you must speak for yourself.

I'll do my best.

That is all anyone can ask. Come.

Mina walked behind Copper as he led her through the glass tunnels, twisting and sloping deeper underground. They paused outside two towering glass doors, but Mina wasn't able to see anything on the other side. Her reflection stared back at her, and she took a deep breath to steady her racing heart.

Copper pressed the top of his head against one of the doors and closed his eyes. A few seconds passed, and then a creaking sound echoed off the walls as the doors slowly swung open. On the other side of the threshold was a massive cavern. Seven dragons were there waiting, all of them as large as Copper.

He walked inside, but Mina stood rooted in place. Dragon fear had consumed her. She trembled uncontrollably, her eyes fixed ahead where a silver dragon sat. The dragon returned her stare unblinkingly. It was a female. Mina could sense her through the scale. The dragon was probing her mind. Hundreds of memories of her past flashed before her eyes within seconds.

The dragon's presence receded from her mind, taking the fear with it.

Mina swallowed hard and stepped into the cavern, taking her place beside Copper. All the elders were watching her, and they filled the chamber with a chaotic wave of scents, but two stood out the strongest: vanilla and freesia.

Why do your emotions have smells to them?

Copper tilted his head to the side, flicking his gaze at her. *We will talk about that later.*

She could feel his astonishment through the scale. Why was he surprised? She turned her attention to the silver dragon in the center. The platform she rested on was taller than the others, and Mina assumed she was the leader of the Enclave.

Step forward.

Mina hesitantly stepped in front of Copper. She was tempted to cast her eyes to the ground, but she forced herself to keep her head up. She could feel all the dragons through the scale, their various presences unique and distinct from one another.

Tiarna, she greeted. *Thank you for honoring me with an audience.*

She felt odd talking like a noble, but Copper had stressed the importance of her words. She bowed at the waist and held the position, counting to three in her mind before rising back up.

It has been a long time since there has been a rider among us, the silver dragon said. *I hope that this is a good thing.*

The other dragons echoed their agreement, their voices swirling together within her mind.

Your bonded tells me you wanted to speak to us about something important?

Yes, Tiarna.

Speak your mind, rider.

Mina wasn't sure why the dragon was calling her a rider. She'd only rode on Copper's back once, and it wasn't something she thought she would do again. She was getting sidetracked, and she knew it.

Copper told me you are going to war against Lord D'Lance. I have come before you to beg you to reconsider. I know that he has perverted the bond, forcing humans and dragons together using dark magic, but many lives will be lost if you take this course.

The dragons remained silent, so she continued.

I learned that we used to be allies. If that is true, do you not think that war is too harsh a punishment? One man's crimes should not weigh upon the innocent.

Collateral damage is always a problem with war, the dragon admitted. *Yet what would you have us do? He must be stopped. Not only has he corrupted the bond, but he is also performing twisted experiments with dragon eggs.*

Mina grimaced. *I did not know that. What kind of experiments?*

The silver dragon looked at Copper. He lowered his head, and they shared a knowing look. The dragon looked back at her.

He is using his magic to manipulate the eggs, combining their life force with humans. He is making himself an army of monsters.

Why didn't you tell me that? Mina asked Copper.

Would it have mattered?

She supposed it wouldn't have, but she didn't like being surprised.

Please, Mina begged the silver dragon. *I am afraid that war will cause more problems than it will solve. If you do this, there's no telling what might happen. People might band together and hunt down dragons.*

Do you think this is something new? It is not. Humans have hunted our kind for ages. You yourself have been responsible for the death of many of my brethren.

Mina's throat constricted and her heart felt like it plummeted into her stomach.

You are right, she said. *I led death to the door of many dragons, but I was naïve and didn't know what I do now. I can't take back my actions, but I hope that I can repair the damage I've done in some way.*

We shall see.

Do not go to war, Mina begged again.

Lord D'Lance must be stopped.

I will stop him.

Her mind went silent. The dragons kept their eyes on her, but their words and emotions eluded her. Their faces were impassive, devoid of any telltale signs that she could decipher. The silence stretched until she thought she'd gone deaf.

What makes you think you can stop him? Powerful men surround him, and his magic is as dark as the night. Are you a warrior, that you will raise a sword against him? No. I have seen your memories. You are not a fighter.

Then I will learn to be one.

Who will teach you?

I'll find someone, Mina said.

The dragon growled and looked at the other elders. They grumbled back and forth, speaking to each other in a way that Mina didn't understand. Finally, the rumbling ceased and the silver dragon looked at her.

We will hold off our attack. You will have two weeks to learn to be a warrior, and then you must deal with Lord D'Lance. If you fail, then we will have our war.

And if I don't fail?

We shall see.

4

Caden sat beside a stream, his bare feet in the water. The temperature was frigid and numbed his skin, which eased the pain of his blisters. Now that he had put some distance between himself and the source of the voice, the entire encounter felt like a dream. If it wasn't for the constant presence of the voice in the back of his mind, he would believe it *had* been a dream.

His stomach growled, reminding him that he needed to find food. He had no idea how long he'd been lying in the burned field before gaining consciousness. Had it been hours or days? Judging by how empty his stomach felt, he guessed the latter. He was in the heart of the woods, so finding game would be easy. Catching it, however, would be the challenge.

The smell of something cooking reached his nose, and he pulled his feet from the water and slipped his boots back on. He stood, strapping his sword belt on, and listened for sounds. At first, there was nothing, and he assumed that the smell must have been the workings of his imagination.

Then he heard voices.

Caden rested his hand on the hilt of his blade and slowly stalked along the trees, following the sound of hushed conversation. Water squished between his toes, making a wet sucking sound with every step. He slowed his pace as he came around a thick cluster of bushes.

A group of men were gathered around a fire. He counted five of them, all wearing armor and armed with a range of weapons. They also had hooded cloaks on, and Caden wondered why they would wear them with the heat. It wasn't as hot as the desert, but wearing a cloak in this weather was still too much.

As he listened, he realized the men were Lord D'Lance's. They spoke low, but he made out the man's name a few times. One of them was tending to an animal that was cooking over the fire. His stomach rumbled again, and the smell tempted him to join them. It was unlikely they would know who he was, especially since he was thought to be dead, but he didn't think it was worth the risk.

Caden turned to leave and found himself cornered by three men. At least, their stature implied they were men. Their faces proved otherwise. They had long snouts like a lizard, and their flesh was scaly. Caden blinked, not sure if what he saw was real. The one closest to him stepped closer.

"What'sss are you doings here?" His tone was low, almost like a whisper.

"I was just passing through," Caden replied. He couldn't take his eyes off the man's face.

"He's lying," another said.

"A spy," chimed the third.

"Comes to see what our master has done? You sees now, don'ts you?"

Caden took a step back, but the lizard man quickly grabbed onto his arm, pulling him close. Caden tried to break away, but the man's grip was solid. The other two closed in and they subdued him, forcing his arms behind his back and binding his wrists.

"Stops yer fighting," the leader-apparent snapped, punching Caden in the stomach.

The blow forced the air from his lungs, and he gasped, falling limp. The lizard men grabbed him by the arms and lifted him, carrying him to where the others were and dropped him to the ground. They began talking to one another in a harsh-sounding language. Caden fought to breathe, temporarily ignored as his captors talked among themselves. Finally, the one that punched him knelt at his side and looked him in the eyes.

"We're goings to eats you," he said.

"You can't," Caden huffed.

"We cans and we wills."

"I'm one of Lord D'Lance's Runesmen. You can't eat me."

The lizard man frowned and rolled Caden onto his stomach, his clawed hands scratching at his neck as he searched for the rune. The creature made a noise that sounded like a curse and began talking with his fellows again. Another of the creatures came and checked the rune for himself, then snorted.

"Two runes. He isss a spy. We will eats him."

"Lord D'Lance will punish you severely if you eat me," Caden said. "He's waiting for me to return to the castle."

The two lizard men exchanged glances, and for a moment, Caden held onto the hope that they were going to release him. The one that noticed both of his runes drew a dagger from a sheath at his waist and pressed the blade to Caden's neck.

"We eats him. Lord D'Lance won'ts knows."

That seemed to excite the entire lot of them, for they began whooping. Caden cursed his luck, and in the back of his mind, he found their existence difficult to fathom. They were like something out of a nightmare, a mix between giant lizards and humans.

A horn blared, and the creatures drew their weapons and looked around worriedly. Caden offered a silent prayer of thanks, thinking that a patrol had found them. Several figures rushed into view, and the clash of arms filled the air. Caden tried to roll away from the fighting, but he only managed to get stuck on his back.

He watched the two groups battle it out and realized that his rescuers weren't human either. They were the same lizard-like men as his captors. Why were they fighting with each other? Was he in more trouble now than before?

The attackers made quick work of his captors,

and bodies littered the makeshift camp. Caden closed his eyes and laid still, hoping these new creatures would think he was dead. He felt one of them standing over him, and curiosity drove him to peek his eyes open.

"He's alive," a rumbling voice said. "You're safe now, my Lord."

Caden was confused. Was the creature referring to him? It knelt and rolled him over, untying his bonds, and then easily pulled him to his feet.

"Our master told us you were in trouble," the creature said.

"What are you talking about?"

"The master that we both serve. She resides in the mountain and has given you authority over her forces. We are small in number now, but we are growing daily. I am Bast."

The voice. That's who he was referring to. The creature spoke flawlessly, unlike the ones who'd captured him.

"Thank you for helping me, Bast."

"It is my duty and an honor, my Lord."

"Just … call me Caden."

"As you command."

"Our master has given me a task that requires entering Lord D'Lance's castle. Is that something you can help me with?"

Bast's lips curled into what looked like a snarl,

but Caden realized he was smiling.

"I know of secret entrances. We will get you inside."

"Excellent."

They stared at one another in silence. Caden had many questions, but he didn't know how to ask them without offending the creature.

"You do not need to fear us," Bast said.

"I'm not afraid, just curious."

"You want to know what we are?"

Caden nodded.

"We were once men like you … until Lord D'Lance changed us."

"How did he change you?"

Caden's stomach grumbled.

"Food first. While you eat, I will tell you what happened."

5

Who was going to train her?

The question plagued Mina as she sat on the floor of Copper's chamber, waiting for him to return. The Enclave had dismissed her and asked him to remain behind, which only added to her worries.

She doubted Lord Klodian would educate her on how to be a soldier, and Thais was questionable. Caden would be her ideal teacher, but he was in the Dracan Dominion now. Did he know that he was serving such a wicked man? That was another fear added onto her already full plate.

Mina was pacing the cavern when Copper finally joined her. She looked at him questioningly.

Your doubt surrounds you like a thick cloud, he said.

I can't help it. I have no idea how I'm going to learn enough in two weeks, but the biggest problem is I don't know anyone who can train me.

Then it is a good thing I do.

You do? Who is it?

Me.

Mina waited for him to laugh, but he only stared at her in silence.

How will you train me to be a warrior? Do

dragons use swords and armor?

No, but my previous rider did. We dragons have an excellent memory, and I am confident that I can teach you what you need to know to fight and survive.

She didn't like it, but at this point, it was her only choice. She nodded.

It looks like I'll have to trust you.

As well you should. We are bonded, and therefore we must have trust in one another. You gave me your word that you would not lead Lord Klodian to any more dragons, and you have kept it.

Your trust only stretches so far, Mina said. *I don't even know your real name.*

Copper snorted. *When you prove to the Enclave that you are a warrior, I will tell you my name.*

I won't fail. I can't.

I believe you. In your chamber, you will find a suit of armor and a sword. Get them and we will begin your training.

Now? Mina asked.

Yes. Two weeks isn't much time, so every moment counts.

He had a point. Mina got up and hurried through the tunnel into her room. She stood before the manakin that had the armor, her hands trembling. Was she ready for this? She wanted to believe that she was, but doubt assailed her. Even if she could learn to use a sword, would she have the fortitude to strike someone down with it?

She didn't know the answer to that. Not yet, at least.

It took her a moment to figure out how to put the armor on, but once she did, she felt different somehow. Stronger, if that made any sense. Copper had mentioned there was a sword as well, but Mina didn't see it. She scoured the room and finally found it atop the wardrobe. A thin layer of dust covered it, and she brushed it off with her fingers, careful not to cut herself.

The blade was smooth and gleamed as if it were new. She strapped the sheath around her waist and returned to Copper's chamber.

You remind me of Lucius, he said.

Was this his armor?

No, but the design is similar. How does it fit?

It's perfect, I think. I've never worn any before. It feels weird.

You'll get used to it. For now, the only time you'll remove it is when you sleep.

And what about later? she asked.

That depends on what happens with Lord D'Lance, but you'll probably have to wear it at all times to be safe.

Mina couldn't imagine trying to sleep in the armor. It wasn't uncomfortable, but it was tight and somewhat constricting.

Do I really need the sword right now?

Yes, Copper replied. *We're going to do some practice while flying.*

Wouldn't it be easier to learn on the ground?

It would, but if you can learn to fight from my back, then fighting on the ground will be a breeze under your wings.

Mina lifted her arms and flapped them playfully. Copper chortled in response, and it made her giggle.

Come, he said. *We're going above ground.*

She followed his lead, admiring the sights as they walked. The large tunnels were much less confusing than the maze of Klodian Keep, and she was confident that she would memorize them quickly. Thinking about the castle made her feel oddly homesick. It was a strange emotion, considering she'd grown up as a slave there. She supposed it was the familiarity of the place, the certainty of what was expected of her.

Here among dragons, she didn't know what to do. Copper was her only friend … if that was what she could call him. He was a stranger to her as much as Thais was, if not more so. Mina watched the dragon as he walked. His stride reminded her of a cat, particularly the way his shoulders rose and fell, and his leathery wings rustled with every step.

As they stepped out of the cave and into daylight, the sun momentarily blinded Mina. She blinked several times until her eyes adjusted.

Sit on my back the way you did when we came here, Copper said.

Is there a saddle we could use? It would be safer with one, wouldn't it?

Nothing about your training is going to be easy.

Mina hesitated. She wanted to learn, but at what cost? Pushing her doubts aside, she climbed onto Copper's back and situation herself. The dragon flapped his wings and leaped into the air, gaining altitude. Once they were high above the ground, Copper wheeled around in large circles.

You will learn the basics first, he said. *While we are flying, you must be aware of the wind. Gusts can spring up suddenly, and they can push you off of my back. If you fall, there's no guarantee I'll be able to catch you.*

That's comforting, Mina replied glumly.

Are you afraid of heights?

I don't think so. Flying here didn't bother me.

Good. Draw your sword.

Mina awkwardly pulled on the hilt of the blade until it came free of the scabbard. It was heavy, and she wondered how she could swing it accurately, let alone wield it in a fight.

Take a practice swing, Copper said.

What if I hit you?

I'll be fine.

Mina stretched her arm out and swung the blade

in a forward chopping motion. Her eyes widened as the hilt slipped from her fingers and the sword went tumbling end over end through the air.

I dropped it, she said.

Copper laughed and dove, streaking through the sky until the ground drew close, then he stretched his wings to catch the air. He landed in the sand and Mina jumped down, running over to where the sword was. It had landed tip down and stood up out of the ground like a relic of bygone days. She pulled it free and carried it back to Copper.

Sorry. It was heavier than I thought.

There's nothing to apologize for. You'll build the strength necessary to keep your grip on it.

Mina doubted she'd be able to make that much progress in two weeks, but she didn't want to give up. She got back on the dragon and waited until they were airborne to try swinging it again. Just as before, the blade jerked free and went spinning to the ground.

It was going to be a long day.

6

Caden watched the lizard men with a wary eye as he chewed on some meat. Bast had cut him a piece from the animal that had been roasting over the fire. The creatures were a lot like normal men with their mannerisms and personalities, but their scaled flesh and elongated faces defied that assumption.

"What do you know of dragons?" Bast asked.

"Not much," Caden replied, shrugging. "They're just wild animals."

"I thought that once, too. I can tell you with certainty that nothing could be further from the truth."

"What do you mean?"

"They aren't mindless creatures. They have intelligent thoughts and they can speak."

Caden rose his left brow. "They can speak?"

"Yes," Bast answered. "I see the doubt on your face. How is it that you can see me and my brethren and know that our existence shouldn't be possible, yet you balk at the idea that dragons can communicate?"

"You make a good argument."

"You don't know, do you?"

"Know what?"

"Our master … she is a dragon."

The image of the glowing eyes behind the throne came to the forefront of his mind, and Caden realized Bast was telling the truth. It made sense looking back now, especially since the source of the voice hadn't come into the light.

"I believe you," he said.

Bast's nostrils flared as he breathed in sharply. "Her scent is on you. Did you get to stand in her presence?"

"I did."

"You hold a high honor. I have not seen her with my own eyes. I have only heard her voice in my mind."

"You said you were all men like me. What happened?" Caden wanted to know more about these lizard men and what their purpose was. If Lord D'Lance was doing more than staging a rebellion, the High Prince would have a much bigger problem on his hands.

"We were not Runesmen like you, but we were loyal soldiers. He came to us with a proposition, one that he wasn't entirely forthcoming about. After we agreed, he changed us. I didn't know it then, but he practices dark magic. The stuff outlawed by the High Prince. He melded us with the energy from dragon eggs. We are both man and dragon. A chaotic existence. Our master calls us draman."

"That's horrible," Caden said. "Why did you agree to it?"

"That is the part that Lord D'Lance left out. He promised us strength and power without the need of a rune. He never told us *how* he would manage the feat."

"What about the ones you attacked? They didn't seem as bright as you."

"My brethren and I were among the first that he transformed. Once we realized what he'd done, we rebelled and fled the castle. We've been hiding in the woods, slowly growing as our master collects more of us. Lord D'Lance started making his newer creations less … intelligent."

"You keep saying brethren. Are you related, or do you consider yourselves family?"

"My apologies. That's the dragon part of me speaking. All dragons are brethren, or family, if you will. The different colors don't get along, but that is a trivial issue when it comes to eradication."

Caden frowned. "Lord D'Lance wants to kill off the dragons?"

"No," Bast replied. "He wants to use dragons as his slaves. He's forcing them to bond with humans while stealing their eggs and making more soldiers. Dragons don't lay many eggs and it can take years for them to hatch. If he isn't stopped, he might cause the extinction of dragons."

You must not let him succeed.

The voice echoed in Caden's mind. He nodded to himself and stood, wandering over to the stream to wash his hands. For some reason he couldn't explain, there was a horrible feeling in the pit of his stomach when he thought about his master dying. He knew nothing about her, certainly not enough to warrant concern, and yet he felt it as surely as he felt the water on his hands. But why?

It was something he would have to think about. He returned to his spot next to Bast and let his hands air dry as he considered the task before them. If Bast could get him into the castle unnoticed, he was confident that retrieving the stone would be relatively easy.

"How many men do you have?" he asked.

"Just under two hundred."

Caden blinked. Two hundred men did not equate to much of an army. Still, it was better than nothing.

"You look disappointed," Bast said.

"It's an obstacle we'll need to overcome."

"Our master is gathering dragons who are not enslaved by Lord D'Lance, and they will bolster our forces greatly."

Caden didn't doubt that, but unless their headcount grew exponentially, it would be a suicide mission trying to battle directly with Lord D'Lance's forces. Their situation was dire, and unless some miracle presented itself, he didn't know how they would succeed. The presence of the voice whispered in the back of his mind, comforting him.

"We need a way of getting more of your

brethren to join us. Why are they defecting?"

"The newer ones aren't as smart, but they still know that they aren't natural creations. And I've heard that he is harsher with his punishments when it comes to their failures. No one wants to be brutalized."

"Perhaps we can use that to our advantage," Caden said, the wheels in his mind turning. "If more of them see what he's doing, they might break ties with him."

"I think you're right," Bast replied. "What are you thinking?"

"It'll be risky, but we can send the newest defectors back to the castle. They can cause a scene, something that will get them punished. If I know Lord D'Lance, he'll want to parade them through the street before executing them publicly."

Bast's eyes turned to slits. "He will kill them, but not in the open. He doesn't let us mingle with anyone. I dare say that none of the nobles are even aware of what he's doing."

"That poses a problem. What about the patrol that captured me? They were in the open."

"He lets us patrol the countryside freely. We don't wear his emblem, therefore no one can tie us back to him if we're seen."

"What if the defectors reveal themselves? They show their faces and start telling everyone what he's doing in secret. He'd have to take action then."

"That is risky," Bast said. "I will talk to my brethren and see if any of them are willing."

Caden nodded. "Good. If we have volunteers, then this should work. They can cause a raucous and gather a crowd. When Lord D'Lance sweeps in and tries to kill them, we'll bring everyone we've got to stop him. The only problem I foresee is that unless your brethren see him using force against the defectors, they won't know the extent of his cruelty."

"Leave that to us. We will spread the word that something big is coming. My brethren will find a way to watch it, and when they do, it should sway them to join us."

"I need to get inside the castle before all of this happens. Our master requires something that he has, so we'll need to make sure we have it in hand first. The sooner, the better."

"We can go tonight. It will give my brethren time to consider the risks, but I'm confident I know what the answer will be."

Caden had the feeling that what they were plotting could very well start a war. That was what Lord D'Lance wanted anyway, but would he still want it if he had to fight dragons?

7

Mina's fingers were sore, and her hand throbbed painfully, yet Copper pushed her onward. The wind plucked at her clothes as she stood on his back, knees bent to keep her low. Her lips were chapped from the wind and sun, and her eyes were so dry that she could barely keep them open.

When can we take a break?

When you can swing the sword correctly, Copper rumbled.

He wasn't being harsh with her, but she was exhausted and his persistence was irritating her. Although they had only been practicing for a few hours, her energy level was flagging. Her stomach felt hollow and her throat was parched. If she lived long enough to get some food, it would be no minor miracle.

Don't be so dramatic. As a rider, you will often go long periods without food or water. You must acclimate your body because things will not always go smoothly.

Mina gritted her teeth against the pain and focused on the image that Copper pushed into her mind. It was of Lucius, his previous rider. He was in a crouched stance, sword at the ready. She was in the same position, but whereas he appeared comfortable and practiced, she felt awkward. The image became animated, and Mina replicated

Lucius's movements.

She twisted her wrist, bringing the blade forward. Her grip on the hilt was as tight as she could get it, and the sword remained in her hand. A wave of excitement washed over her. She did it!

Good, Copper said. *You didn't drop your weapon. Let's try something different. Run along my back to my tail.*

Why?

Just do it.

Mina tightened her grip on the sword and slowly turned around. The ridges and spines on his back provided an uneven terrain, but she reminded herself that she needed to trust him. She inhaled a deep breath and sprinted, her ankles jerking sharply with each step. As she reached his tail, she slowed her pace.

What now?

Keep going!

She did as Copper said. As she reached the thinnest part of his tail, he undulated it, sending her flying into the air. Her eyes widened as she rose higher, and she windmilled her arms, letting go of the sword. Time stilled as she hovered in the air. Copper's tail faded from view, and then she was falling. She screamed in terror as her stomach flip-flopped.

The wind whipped violently, buffeting her as she streaked toward the ground. Mina closed her eyes and cursed Copper, wondering why she had allowed herself to trust him. Suddenly, her fall broke. The air was forced from her lungs and she opened her eyes, struggling to breathe. She had landed on Copper's back. Or rather, he had caught her. Instinctively, she grabbed onto his scales and held on. Copper spiraled in wide circles as he slowly descended.

You tried to kill me!

I did no such thing, Copper retorted. *It was a lesson.*

A lesson in near-death experiences?

The dragon laughed, but Mina didn't find the situation funny at all.

I wanted to show you what can happen if you fall off my back. I was able to easily catch you, but if we were battling in the sky, it would be almost impossible. Now that you know the feeling of free falling, you will remember the importance of keeping your balance.

Mina thought it was an incredibly dangerous way to teach such a simple lesson. She silently fumed until they landed, and then she leaped off his back and trudged across the sand to the cave entrance. Copper didn't follow her, for which she was thankful. She made it to Copper's chamber with little difficulty and stripped her armor and clothes off, then climbed into the pool of water.

Judging by the sting of her flesh, she'd received a decent sunburn. The water cooled her off, and she sighed with relief. She was tempted to drink some of it, but she didn't think that was a good idea. Who knew what sorts of germs were floating unseen, especially in a dragon's cave.

She got out and air-dried, then put her clothes back on. She left the armor on the ground and went back above ground. Copper was basking in the sun, his wings outstretched.

I did not intend to upset you, he said.

He *had* upset her, but she shrugged in reply. Serving under Lord Klodian, she'd learned many things, such as how to control her emotions. Her wall of stoicism had cracked and her anger had slipped through. Guilt assailed her.

I'm sorry for overreacting, she said.

You didn't overreact. It is natural for your emotions to affect you in such ways. You felt that I put you in danger. Your anger was justified. I will give you more warning next time.

Mina stared at him for a moment before nodding.

I'm hungry, she said, changing the subject.

You will find food in your room. Two meals will be prepared each day.

Only two?

Yes. Humans are frivolous in their consumption. You will only eat what is necessary.

What about water?

Copper's eyes glinted in the sun as he tilted his head.

I will show you where to drink. I think you will find it ... interesting.

He retracted his wings and walked past her, leading the way back into the cave. They followed the tunnel that bypassed their chambers and continued. The ground sloped under Mina's feet, and she could tell they were going deeper underground. At one point, the light that flickered within the glass walls faded.

Grab hold of my tail, Copper said.

Mina did as he asked and trailed blindly behind him. The darkness was impenetrable, but despite her discomfort, she wasn't afraid. They walked a few hundred feet before a faint glow appeared ahead. Mina released Copper's tale and moved beside him. The light was coming from a giant green stone that was lodged in the ceiling. It was multi-faceted and smooth.

What is that?

It's a crystal, Copper replied. *We found it when we were building our home here.*

Does magic make it glow like that?

Not everything is magical. It glows naturally.

The tunnel opened up to a crescent-shaped ledge. High above, but below the crystal, a waterfall cascaded down the left wall, filling a large pool with clear liquid.

This water is safe for you to drink, Copper said. *It is filtered by the sand and rocks.*

Mina knelt at the ledge and cupped her hands, dipping them into the water. She brought them back up quickly and drank. The water was cold and refreshing. Copper waited patiently while she drank her fill, and when she was finished, they trekked through the tunnel and returned to his chamber.

You can eat now, and when you are ready, we will practice with the sword again.

I dropped it when you tossed me into the air, so I'll have to find it.

I retrieved the weapon when you stormed off.

Oh. Thank you.

Mina left Copper's chamber and went into her own. A tray of steaming food was waiting for her. As she dug into it, she paused to wonder who had made it. A shuffling sound came from the shadows, startling her. She peered in the direction of the noise and saw two glowing eyes. Copper was only a few feet away if she needed him, so she wasn't too worried.

"Who's there?" she asked.

"It me," a soft voice replied. The tone was light, almost musical.

"Me who?"

"Me. It me."

"Step out of the shadows so I can see you."

The shuffling sound repeated, and a diminutive creature stepped into the light. It was roughly three feet tall, and at first, Mina thought it was a child. As she took in the creature's appearance, it became clear that it wasn't. In fact, it wasn't even human. It had a pale complexion, a bald head, and pointed ears.

There's something in here, Mina told Copper.

What is it?

I don't know.

Mina felt Copper's presence within her mind intensify.

Ah. That's Areg. Don't be afraid of him. He's harmless.

"It me," Areg repeated, pointing to himself.

"Your name is Areg?"

The creature nodded.

"What are you doing in my chamber?"

"Bring food. You eat."

"Oh. Thank you."

"Me serve you. If need, pull rope."

Areg pointed to the doorway that led into the hall, and Mina realized there was a rope that hung down from the ceiling.

"I will let you know if I need anything."

Areg attempted a bow, but it looked more like he was about to fall over. He righted himself and then hobbled out of the room.

What is Areg? He walks on two legs, but I've never seen anything like him before.

Areg is an elf, Copper replied.

Mina had heard of them before, but only in stories. She never thought that they could be real. With each new thing she learned, it became more and more apparent that the world of dragons was much different from what she ever imagined.

8

The moon glowed overhead as Caden followed Bast through the woods toward Velbridge. A few stray beams of light penetrated the canopy, but Caden still found it difficult to see the way ahead. Bast, on the other hand, strode with sure steps.

"You have some good eyes," Caden said.

"There are some benefits to what Lord D'Lance has done to me, but they are few."

"I still can't believe he's done something so unholy. No offense."

"None taken," Bast replied. "Some days are harder than others, but it's a constant struggle to know who I am. The humanity battles against the dragon, and they are never at peace."

Caden couldn't imagine an existence like that, and he admired the man's fortitude. They trekked for a few hours, and by the time they reached the outskirts of the city, it was past midnight. Bast led him along the eastern wall, stopping at a large grate that covered a tunnel. A thin rivulet of sickly green water streamed out of it and into a trench that directed it away from the city. Caden wrinkled his nose.

"The sewers?"

"It's disgusting, but it's the safest way inside the city without attracting attention. Guards don't patrol them, so we'll have little trouble until we come back above ground. I'll need your help to open the grate."

Between the two of them, they were able to jerk the rusted grate open enough to get inside. It was rectangular in shape, and the tunnel was low and narrow.

"We'll leave this open," Bast said.

"Won't that draw attention?"

"I think that's unlikely. We need to have a quick way of escape in case something goes wrong. There are too many guards to risk going out of the main gates."

Caden didn't like it, but he didn't have a better idea.

"How close can we get to the castle?"

"There's an exit on the western side that will bring us into Lord D'Lance's private garden. From there, we can use a secret passage to get inside. The only problem is that because of its proximity to Lord D'Lance's personal quarters, they usually pack the place with soldiers. We'll have to use caution to ensure we aren't caught."

"If we're able to get that close to his quarters, why not just sneak in and kill him in his sleep?"

"That would not be prudent," Bast said. "Our master desires to spill his blood herself."

Caden remembered that she'd told him not to touch Lord D'Lance. He nodded. "We're going to need a torch."

"No, we won't. I can see as plain as day in the darkest room. Just follow me."

Bast stepped into the tunnel, and Caden trailed after him. A few feet in and the darkness was absolute. Caden's steps were hesitant, so Bast grabbed his hand and pulled him along. He felt awkward holding hands with the draman, but he forced the feeling aside. They had a task to complete, and he would not let a minor discomfort get in the way.

Caden assumed the sewers would be a quiet place, but that was far from the truth. The sound of flowing water and scurrying creatures echoed off the walls. Every time they splashed through a puddle, he was glad he was wearing boots. The thought of that water touching him made his skin crawl with revulsion.

The sewer tunnels were a confusing labyrinth and reminded him of the interior of Lord Klodian's castle, but it wasn't long before they stopped. Overhead, faint light shone through a circular grate.

"There are rungs in the wall," Bast said, guiding Caden's hand to one. "They are slippery, so climb slowly. I'll go up first to make sure it's clear."

Bast ascended them quickly. In the dim light, it looked to Caden as though the draman was scaling the wall itself rather than using the metal rungs. He reached the top and pushed the grate aside, then stuck his head into the open.

"All clear," he whispered.

Caden made his way up slowly. Condensation had collected on the rungs, making them slick, and he had to be meticulous with how he placed his hands and feet. Bast had already exited the tunnel by the time Caden reached the top.

"Over here." Bast waved.

Caden spotted the draman hiding in some tall shrubs that rested against the castle. He cast a glance around the garden and didn't see any guards, so he climbed out and hurried to where Bast was.

"Step lightly and try not to jostle the bushes."

Bast pressed his back against the stonework and began sidestepping through the slim space between the shrubbery and the castle. Caden did the same thing, doing his best to creep without noise, but it was difficult because loose stones covered the ground. It seemed to take an eternity, but finally, Bast held up his left hand and placed a finger from his right one to his lips.

"Two guards," he murmured. "They are in front of the entrance."

"Do they know it's there?"

"I don't think so. We need some way of getting them to leave."

"I've got an idea," Caden said.

He knelt and felt around blindly with his hand until he found what he was looking for: a palm-sized rock. He hurled it up through the bush and, a moment later, it clattered in the distance.

"What was that?" one of the soldiers asked.

"How should I know? It's my turn to roll, so go check it out. It's probably a critter."

The first soldier grumbled and headed in the direction of Caden's stone. The other was sitting on the ground in front of a small wooden square. Behind him, a lantern hung upon a post and offered a small amount of light to see by. The soldier held his hand over the board and dropped two dice onto it. He cursed under his breath and looked for his fellow, then flipped the dice over and grinned.

"We need them both gone," Bast whispered.

Before Caden could reply, the other guard returned.

"I didn't see anythin'. Hey! What's this, then? There's no way you rolled a double six. Are you cheating?"

"I ain't never cheated a day in my life," the other guard sputtered.

"I doubt that!"

"Are you callin' me a liar?"

"Well, I ain't calling you a truth teller. Roll 'em again while I'm watchin'."

"Bah! Fine."

He picked the dice up and rolled them again. This time, he did roll two sixes.

"Ha! See? I wasn't lyin'."

"We don't have time for this," Caden said.

Bast stared at him. "We can kill them, but we'll have to hide their bodies."

Caden considered the option for a moment and sighed. "No. I don't want to kill innocent men. They probably know nothing about what Lord D'Lance is doing."

"Then what?"

"Do you hear that?" the first guard asked.

"Hear what?"

They both went silent, and Caden and Bast barely breathed.

"I don't hear nothin'. Are you losin' your mind now, too?"

Bast motioned for Caden to stay put and sidled his way through the bushes until he was behind the soldier sitting on the ground. Caden had no idea what the man was up to, but he hoped he wasn't going to kill either of them. Bast rustled the bushes, and the second soldier peered suspiciously into the shadows.

"There's somethin' in there."

"Where?"

"Behind you."

The guard stood up and turned around, retrieving the lantern from the post. He held it out in front of him and shined the light into the bushes. Bast held perfectly still, and neither soldier saw him.

"Must be the wind," the soldier said. He turned back around, and Bast made his move. He rushed forward and wrapped his arm around the soldier's neck, putting him in a chokehold. The other soldier's face went pale, but he drew his sword and took a step toward Bast.

"Let him go or I'll gut you!"

Caden slipped out of the bushes and stealthily moved in behind the man. Bast bared his teeth in a nightmarish grin and released the guard, who crumpled to the ground, unconscious.

"You killed him! Demon spawn!"

Caden kicked the back of the soldier's right leg, buckling his knee. He went down and Caden placed his hand over the man's mouth, pinching his nose closed. The man struggled to get free, but Bast took his sword and pressed the tip to his throat.

"Hold still," he said.

The lantern had fallen to the ground, and the light it cast shined on Bast's face. The guard stopped fighting, and a moment later, Caden laid him on the ground.

"They won't be out long," he said.

"We should hurry, then. Where is the item you seek?"

"I'm not sure, but I know where we can check first."

9

Mina.

Her eyes cracked open. Had someone called her name? She waited a moment, but she didn't hear anything. It must have been one of the servants. Her eyelids slowly descended and she was about to drift back to sleep when she heard it again.

Mina rubbed the sleep from her eyes and sat up, glancing around the room. She frowned in confusion. This wasn't her room. Where was she? And then it all came flooding back, hitting her like a bolt of lightning.

Copper?

Get your armor on and meet me in the hall.

She frowned, not remembering how she'd fallen asleep. Then again, the dragon had pushed her beyond exhaustion. Mina groggily slipped out of bed and was about to retrieve her armor from Copper's chamber when she saw it was on the manakin beside her wardrobe. She paused, her tired mind trying to remember when she'd brought it into her room.

Shrugging, she put the armor on over her clothes and buckled her sword belt around her waist, then stepped into the hall where Copper was waiting.

I'm awake, she said, stifling a yawn. *Well,*

mostly.

Copper laughed. *You fell asleep early. I'm surprised you slept so long. I would have been concerned, but your mind was still present.*

I haven't worked that hard in a long time.

Today won't be any easier. How are you with a bow?

I've never used one, Mina admitted.

Then you shall learn today. An effective rider must know how to wield more than just a sword.

Shouldn't I master one weapon before learning another?

In an ideal situation, yes, but time is not on our side. You must learn many things quickly.

She knew he was right, but she wasn't feeling confident in her ability to learn what was needed.

Come, Copper bade.

They went above ground and Mina realized the sun hadn't quite risen yet. The morning air was cool, and she shivered, rubbing her hands along her upper arms. Areg was there, holding a bow and a quiver of arrows. Dotting the desert landscape around them was a multitude of manakins.

We will fly past the targets, and you will attempt to hit them with an arrow. Are you ready?

Mina rubbed her eyes, still not fully awake. *I suppose I am.*

"Here go."

Areg held the bow out to her and she grabbed hold of it. The wood was a pale honey color and smooth to the touch. The elf handed over the quiver next, and she noticed that each arrow had a thin red ribbon attached.

What are those for? she asked.

In case you miss. It'll be easier to find them. Since you are shooting from my back, that strap on the quiver will go across your chest. If you are on foot, it'll go around your waist.

What's the difference?

Pulling arrows from the quiver on your back is clumsy and only suitable when riding. It's easier and quicker to pull them from your waist when you're on foot. And unless you're wearing strong leather boots, you'll want to be barefoot when firing, otherwise you won't have firm footing.

I'll remember all of this somehow, Mina lamented.

Mastery comes with time. For now, you just need to know the basics. Climb up.

Mina slipped the quiver strap over her head and adjusted it across her chest, then climbed onto Copper's back. She braced herself as he flexed his wings out and leaped into the air, rising quickly. He flew a fair distance away from the area where the targets were before turning back and slowly descending until he was roughly ten feet above the ground, then leveled out.

Ready your bow, he said, projecting an image of

Lucius into her mind.

She pulled an arrow from the quiver, almost dropping it as she tried to fit the end on the bowstring. Copper glided effortlessly over the landscape, but the wind pushed against her, making her unsteady. They were approaching the first target. She took aim and fired. The arrow shot forward a few feet and then whipped away in the opposite direction.

You must pull back on the string harder. More tension.

Mina grabbed another arrow, but before she could nock it to the string, the next target zipped by.

Too slow! Copper grumbled.

I'm trying, Mina retorted.

She caught sight of the third target and aimed again. When it was only a few feet away, she released the string. The arrow flew straight and struck the manakin in the leg.

I did it! Mina shouted excitedly.

Copper remained silent, but she could smell lemon and clove coming off of him. As the rest of the targets came and went, she fired off more arrows as best as she could, but missed all the shots. Copper landed near Areg and Mina jumped down to the ground.

Retrieve the arrows.

Mina jogged across the sand to each target and collected the projectiles, then returned, panting.

Areg will show you how to fire accurately.

Mina looked at the elf and he took the bow from her, along with one arrow.

"Watch."

In one fluid motion, he nocked the arrow, aimed, and let the shaft fly. It whizzed through the air and struck one of the furthest targets.

"Go get," Areg said.

Mina did as he asked and saw that he'd struck the manakin dead center. Her eyes widened in surprise. Areg was so … small. How had he shot the arrow that far? She pulled the arrow free and walked back to where the elf was.

"How did you do that?" she asked.

Areg smiled. "Me do it before."

"What do you mean?"

The elf shook his head and gave her the bow back. He motioned at her, and she nocked the arrow to the string, then looked at him expectantly.

"Now what?"

"Kneel."

She did so, and Areg smacked her elbow.

"Twist," he said, then placed his hand over hers and put his index, middle, and ring finger on the string, keeping the arrow between his index and middle fingers.

"Keep here. No squeeze."

"Don't squeeze the arrow. Got it."

Copper projected another image of Lucius into her mind, and she mirrored his stance. She drew the arrow back to a comfortable spot on her face, at the corner of her mouth.

"Focus," Areg said. "Small."

"I don't understand."

Focus on something small, Copper clarified. *A blemish or something specific on the target. The smaller the better. Keep your eyes on it until everything else becomes a blur, then relax your fingers and let the string slip past them.*

Mina followed the instructions and focused on an odd patch of color on the manakin's shirt. She released the string and the arrow struck the target exactly where she'd aimed. Areg clapped and Copper emitted lemon and clove again.

Very good. Now try to hit every target from here.

She knew it wasn't possible, but tried anyway. Two arrows hit, and the rest were way off mark.

That was impossible.

Perhaps, but you learned how to aim. Let's try from the air again. You don't get breakfast until you can strike all the targets in one go.

Mina gathered the errant projectiles and climbed onto Copper's back. He flew past the targets again, and this time, she didn't hit a single one. He landed so she could collect the arrows again, and she stalked back to him.

Let's go again, she huffed.

10

Caden wasn't very familiar with the castle's interior, especially in the dark. He described the door he'd seen previously, and Bast guided him through the halls. They encountered a few soldiers making their rounds and had to duck into a darkened doorway to avoid being seen. After they guards passed, they continued onward until they reached an empty hall.

"This is it," Caden said. "It's the door at the end."

"I know this place," Bast replied. "I think it is where my transformation happened."

"You're not sure?"

"I was in and out of consciousness, but this area feels familiar. I don't have any memory of it before that point."

Caden strode to the door and tried the handle, but just as it had been before, it was locked.

"You don't remember anything about a key, do you?"

"No."

Nothing could ever be easy, could it? Caden frowned as he stared at the door. They could try to search for a key, but the chances of finding one were so remote it didn't seem worth the effort. It was impossible to know if any of the guards had a key, and if one of them did, who?

"Step aside," Bast said. "Hopefully this isn't too loud."

Caden moved out of the way. Bast took up a stance in front of the door, placing his shoulder against it. He grabbed the handle and jerked it. It broke, and he cast it aside. It clattered along the floor and slid to a stop.

"That didn't go as expected," Bast said. He pushed on the door, but it didn't budge.

"How did you break the handle?"

"I didn't mean to."

"No, I mean *how* did you do it? It's metal."

"Fusing with the dragon egg has increased my strength. Sometimes I use too much force."

"Can you break the door open?"

"Yes, but it may draw the guards on us."

Caden knew he was right, but they had little time. "Do it."

Bast took a few steps back and kicked the door. The wood where the handle had been splintered, and the rest of the door flew inward, slamming loudly against something on the inside. They hurried into the room, and Caden froze at what he saw.

Lying atop a table was a body. The top half was human, but from the waist down, it had scales like Bast's. Strange utensils were laid out next to it, including a vial of black liquid. The human portion had pale skin and a sunken face. It was obvious the person was dead.

"This one didn't survive the process," Bast said, standing next to him.

"What causes them to die?"

"Lord D'Lance hasn't fully mastered the dark magic he uses, and dragons are powerful, even as an unhatched egg. If the dragon fights back, the spell is disrupted and it can kill the person involved. I saw a few survive the failure, but they ended up dying within a couple of days."

"He's more of a monster than I realized."

"He has deceived many, but now is not the time to discuss that. What is it that we are looking for?"

"A gemstone," Caden replied.

"What kind?"

The image of a bright green jadeite formed with Caden's mind. He could sense it was coming from his master, and it impressed him that she could still communicate with him despite their distance.

"It's green, but it's not like an emerald. It's murky looking."

"I don't remember seeing anything like that, but as I said, my memories from the transformation are not cohesive."

"You check this room. I'll look in that one."

He pointed to the doorway at the far end of the

room. Bast began his search, and Caden went to the other room. Inside, there were a dozen tables with the same grisly scene. Half transformed bodies were laid out, their flesh in the beginning stages of decay. Caden pinched his nose against the stench and glanced around.

There was a long table against the back wall that held dragon eggs. At least, he assumed that's what they were. He walked over and inspected them. They varied in size and color, but they were all covered with a dark shade of red, similar to rust. He didn't dare touch them. Aside from the bodies, there wasn't much else to see, so he returned to the room where Bast was. The draman was looking closely at the body on the table.

"Any sign of the stone?"

"No," Bast answered. "But this corpse looks different from the others I've seen. I think Lord D'Lance is experimenting."

"There are eggs with some sort of red dust on them in there."

Bast's reptilian eyes turned to slits, and he growled. "He's up to something."

"We can deal with that later. Right now we need to find the stone, and it doesn't seem to be in here."

"What does this stone do?"

"Our master said that Lord D'Lance is using it to keep her trapped in the mountain. She wants me to find and destroy it."

"If it is valuable to him, he will keep it close. He likely has it in his personal quarters," Bast said.

"We can't leave without it."

The two exchanged looks.

"If the master needs it, then we shall get it. Are you prepared to die if it comes to that?"

"I will do what I must," Caden replied.

"Follow me."

Bast took the lead again and they headed back the way they'd come. Instead of going back out of the secret passage, they turned right and ended up in a large chamber that resembled the Coterie. A plush rug rested in the center of the room and benches lined the walls. The room was dark aside from the meager moonlight that streamed through the windows. A single door offered the only path ahead, but as they approached it, a guard stepped out of the shadows to intercept them.

"What are you two doing in here?"

"Apologies, sir. We've got urgent news for Lord D'Lance," Bast said.

"You can tell me what it is, and I'll inform him personally."

"I'm afraid it's for his ears only, sir."

"Then I'm afraid it will have to wait until morn—" His words turned into a gurgling sound and Bast removed a dagger from the guard's neck. The man clutched at the wound and collapsed to the floor.

"I'm sorry," Bast said, turning to Caden. "I know you said you didn't want to kill anyone, but this one deserved it. He's as cruel as Lord D'Lance."

Caden didn't say anything. He stepped over the body and opened the door. It swung open silently, and the first thing he saw was an enormous bed. Sheer curtains draped the entire thing. Caden crept into the room and quickly rummaged through the drawers of an ornate dresser. Bast went to the desk on the other side of the room, and after a few minutes of searching, he joined Caden.

"Nothing," he whispered.

"Blast our luck," Caden replied. "It must be here somewhere."

He saw a side table beside the bed and hurried over to it, but it was empty. Lord D'Lance was in the bed, his breathing rhythmic and steady. Caden put his hand on the hilt of his sword. It would be so easy to end the tyrant's life. He wanted to, and deep down he knew that he should, but the invisible presence of his master kept him at bay.

His life is mine. Your task is to find the stone.

Forgive my weakness.

Caden was about to continue looking through the room when he saw a silver chain around Lord D'Lance's neck. Pushing the curtain aside, he leaned closer and saw the gemstone. It was encased in a pendant that was affixed to the chain.

"I found it," he whispered, looking at Bast.

"Take it and let's go."

Caden didn't see the clasp, which meant that he either had to pull the chain free or get the gemstone out of the pendant. Neither option was ideal, considering the situation.

"Get ready to run."

Caden gently lifted the chain enough to get a firm grip, then yanked it free. Lord D'Lance's eyes opened and he sat up. He looked from Caden to the pendant, and his brow furrowed.

"Come on!" Bast shouted.

Caden turned to flee, but his legs wouldn't move. He looked at Lord D'Lance and saw the man had ensorcelled him. His hand was balled into a fist, and he was chanting something under his breath.

"I can't move!"

Bast rushed over and tried to pull him, but his legs remained where they were, as if rooted in place. The draman leaped onto the bed and punched Lord D'Lance in the face, breaking his focus on the spell. Caden lurched forward a few steps, but then he was thrown to the ground as Bast crashed into him. They both grunted in pain and struggled to untangle themselves.

"Guards!"

Caden got on all fours and crawled for the door, but an unseen force slammed it shut. He clambered to his feet and looked for another way out. Lord D'Lance was out of his bed, his face twisted with rage. He made a motion with his hand, and the pendant was ripped from Caden's grasp. It flew across the room and Lord D'Lance snatched it out of the air.

"Tell that sniveling dragon that she'll rot in that mountain. She will never be free again."

"She will be free," Bast shouted. "And she'll flame you into oblivion!"

The door burst open, and armed guards filed into the room. Caden and Bast retreated to the window.

"Kill them," Lord D'Lance ordered.

The guards drew their swords and rushed toward them. Bast grabbed Caden and shielded him with his body as he crashed through the glass of the window, stumbling onto a balcony that overlooked the garden.

"Bend your knees and roll," Bast said, then tossed Caden over the edge.

Caden landed on his feet and used his momentum to spring forward, rolling into a bed of flowers. He quickly got up and sprinted for the sewer entrance, Bast right behind him. They reached the hole and climbed down into the sewer, escaping into the night.

11

Mina was awake well before dawn. She paced her chamber anxiously, continuously running her hands over the front of her armor as if to smooth it out. Her nerves were on edge. This day was probably the most important that she'd ever waited for. The last two weeks of training had been arduous, miserable even. It felt like months had passed.

But it was over.

Almost.

She took a deep breath and continued pacing. Copper was recounting his time with her to the Enclave, and upon their approval, they would test her to prove if she was a capable warrior.

A warrior.

Mina almost laughed. Her life was so foreign now. She'd been raised from the position of a slave to a height that she'd never dreamed of.

Copper had pushed her beyond what she'd thought possible. Every day, she woke up before dawn and practiced with the sword, then with the bow, then back to the sword. She had no time to relax, had barely received any personal time to reflect on what she was doing. Now that she had a small amount of free time, she didn't know what to do with herself. And so she paced, her thoughts full of turmoil.

What would happen if she failed? War, obviously. But what about her? What did her fate look like? Scarier still, what did her future hold if she succeeded?

You dwell on things you have no control over, Copper said, his voice invading her mind.

I can't help it. What did the Enclave say?

They want to see what you have learned. Grab your sword and come with me.

Mina's sword was already strapped around her waist, so she stepped into the hall. Copper regarded her in silence.

What troubles you? he asked.

I'm afraid of failing.

Do not fear failure. It is a fire that refines you. Give everything you have in these tests. Whether you fail or succeed, you have done your duty in trying.

I will do my best, Mina swore.

They headed above ground, where the Enclave was waiting for them, as well as a host of other dragons. Mina's breath caught in her throat. There were so many of them, and they were all different colors. Their shiny scales glinted in the sun, creating a myriad of miniature rainbows.

Why are they all out here?

You are the first rider in a thousand years, Copper replied. *It is a momentous event.*

The invisible weight of their judgement and expectations suddenly fell on her shoulders. She hadn't expected so many witnesses. Still, the stakes were clear in her mind. She cast the doubts aside and walked with as much confidence as she could muster.

Mina, step forth and kneel before the Enclave.

It was the silver dragon, the one who'd probed her mind when she'd first arrived. Mina left Copper's side and approached the group of leaders, then knelt in the sand.

Today, we will see what you have learned. Put forth your best efforts. Not only to convince us, but because you are a rider. We are in a unique predicament, and I trust that there is a reason for the bond between the two of you. Do not disappoint us.

Yes, Tiarna.

A tremor shook the sand beneath her feet, and Mina glanced at the members of the Enclave. The dragons looked at each other, and she could smell vanilla drifting off of them. She wrinkled her nose.

Prepare for your trials.

Mina lowered her head briefly and rose to her feet, returning to Copper's side. Areg handed her a bow and a quiver of arrows. She slipped them both over her shoulder and climbed up Copper's foreleg and onto his back.

Did you feel that a moment ago? she asked.

Yes.

What was it?

I don't know.

I smelled vanilla on the elders. What does that mean?

Can you truly smell our emotions?

Yes, Mina answered.

You are one of only a few humans who've been able to do so. I don't know why you have the ability, but it will help create a stronger bond between us. Our emotions release pheromones to other dragons, much like the pheromone that lets us locate one another. In this case, you don't get overwhelmed with fear, but can smell our emotions.

Mina scrunched her brow.

What emotion is vanilla?

Curiosity.

So the elders are curious about the ground tremor?

Possibly, or they may be curious about you. If you cannot decipher the object of their emotion, then you will never know.

Can't you tell me?

I could, but I'm not going to.

Why not?

You need to be focused on the trials you are about to face. Do not worry about these things now.

Mina sighed. *Very well.*

The silver dragon nodded, and Copper leaped into the air. The silver dragon's voice penetrated her mind.

Your first test is archery. You must hit every target.

Mina unslung the bow and grabbed an arrow, readying herself. As Copper gained altitude and the ground below grew distant, she wondered how she would hit the targets at this height. And then she noticed there were other dragons joining them, each one wearing a target on their back.

What's going on? she asked. *What are they doing?*

My brethren bear the targets you must hit.

I have to hit moving *targets? But I've only trained on stationary ones!*

You can hit them, Copper said. *If I didn't think you were capable, then you wouldn't be tested.*

She thought that his confidence was misplaced, but she'd gone through too much to give up now. She inhaled a deep breath and lifted the bow.

I'm ready.

The dragons flying around them broke away, wheeling in different directions. Copper flapped his wings and turned left, following after the closest one. The wind pummeled her, drying out her eyes. She clenched her jaw and kept her legs pressed tightly against Copper as she took aim.

Her first target was on the back of a sleek gold dragon. Mina wasn't sure, but she assumed it was a female judging by the smaller stature of the beast. She drew the string back and held herself as steady as she could, keeping her eyes fixed on the center of the target. The dragon did a barrel roll, causing her to lose focus.

I can't get a good aim because she keeps moving!

Calm yourself, Copper admonished. *Patience is key. Wait for the right moment.*

She refocused on the target and waited. Time slipped by, and she lost count of the seconds. The gold dragon swooped up, and Mina saw her opportunity. She released the bowstring and the arrow whizzed through the sky. It was faint compared to the wind, but she heard the arrow strike the target. The dragon tilted to the side and fell below them, returning to the ground.

A perfect strike. Very good, but don't let it go to your head. You've got plenty more targets, and you must hit them all.

Do I have to hit them on the first try?

Yes.

Mina grabbed another arrow and knocked it. She leaned low as Copper turned and closed in on the next target: a brass dragon twice the size of Copper. His bulk would make it harder for him to maneuver, but it also made the target on his back seem much smaller.

Can you fly over top of him?

Yes, but you won't be able to see the target.

I meant upside down.

She sent an image of what she had in mind through the scale. The brief scent of freesia hit her nostrils, followed by lemon and clove.

Hold on, Copper replied.

Mina clenched her legs against his neck and prepared for the riskiest thing she'd ever attempted.

12

The master wants you to stay behind.

The words echoed within Caden's mind, a reminder of his failure to retrieve the gemstone two weeks earlier. He assumed it was a punishment, and he berated himself daily. If only he'd been more prepared.

Lord D'Lance was hosting a public celebration for the High Prince, and Bast had spent the last few hours finalizing their plans to disrupt the event.

"You seem depressed."

Caden looked up at the draman and laughed. "Disappointed is more like it. I can't lead our master's forces if I'm not with them. I failed the task she gave me, and I know this is my reward."

"I think you misunderstand her," Bast said. "She wants you to stay behind for your safety. If you are killed tomorrow, then we suffer a significant loss. Our numbers have doubled since you arrived, and my brethren are beginning to see that there is hope."

"I hadn't considered that. I suppose I'm being too hard on myself."

"Everyone fails at some point. What you do after that determines your character."

The two of them sat near a small fire, one of many scattered around their camp. Caden was warm and relaxed, and he watched the flames dance about. Perhaps Bast was right. The master wanted him to stay behind to keep him safe, not to punish him. The thought did comfort him, at least until he dwelled on his men going into a possible death trap alone. How could he call himself a leader if he wasn't in the thick of danger with them?

"What's the point of hosting a party for the High Prince if he won't even be attending?"

"To the people, it's a show of support," Bast said. "And to the High Prince, it's a sign of loyalty."

"I've heard it said that the High Prince has eyes and ears everywhere. What are the chances that Lord D'Lance's plot has already reached him?"

"It's possible. If he does know, I wonder why he hasn't marched his army out to destroy Velbridge."

Caden had wondered about that, too. There were many answers, but he feared it was because either the High Prince was too proud to admit one of his lords would betray him, or that Lord D'Lance had become too powerful to stop. The latter idea was the most concerning.

"So far, Lord D'Lance has kept his dragons and draman a secret, but I don't think that's going to last much longer."

"Especially not after tomorrow," Bast said with a grin.

"You're still leaving before dawn?"

"Yes. My brethren are ready. I will leave some

men behind to guard you while we are away. A line of messengers will also be in place to alert you if something happens. You'll have plenty of time to escape to the mountain if we are compromised."

"You're a capable leader," Caden complimented. "I have no doubt you'll be fine."

"Thank you. As long as Lord D'Lance's dragons do not make an appearance, I think all will go according to plan. We've been spreading the word, and I am confident that the rest of our brethren will see the truth and join us."

"Let us hope so. You should get some rest. Tomorrow is an important day."

"I am excited, but you are right." Bast stood and stretched, his scales shimmering softly under the firelight. "We shall meet again tomorrow after the dust has settled."

Caden stayed by the fire after he left, battling with his own thoughts. Their master hadn't told him directly to stay behind, so if he followed his men to Velbridge, he wouldn't be disobeying her orders.

Technically.

And it wasn't like Bast was his commander. They led the band of draman together. He laid down and got comfortable, staring up at the dark canopy. The more he thought about it, the more he convinced himself to tag along in secret. He wouldn't get involved … he would just keep an eye on things.

He awoke early in the morning as the draman

were preparing to travel to Velbridge. They weren't a quiet lot, and it was impossible for him to go back to sleep even if he wanted to. Bast bid him farewell and led the men away from the camp.

Caden waited as patiently as he could, allowing them a head start before going after them. The few guards left behind weren't paying him any heed, and he grabbed a discarded cloak and a torch, then snuck off into the woods. He kept a fair distance behind Bast and the others, and once Velbridge was in sight, he turned to the east and used the sewer entrance Bast had showed him to enter the city.

He used the torch to light his way, and since he wasn't familiar with the tunnels, he decided to keep straight until he reached a fork, then turned right and climbed up the first set of rungs he found. The grate slid aside easily and he exited into an empty alleyway.

Cheering echoed off the walls, and Caden realized the celebration was already underway. He pulled the hood of the cloak over his head and doused the torch, tossing it aside, then stepped into the street and made his way toward the festivities. The streets were normally crowded, but with the event happening, he only encountered a handful of people, stragglers who were going the same direction he was.

It was only midmorning, but it amazed him to see how big the crowd was that had flocked to the front of the castle. The people were packed close together, all trying to get a good view of what was happening. Caden scaled the side of a building and got on the rooftop. A parade of sorts was passing through the primary thoroughfare, blocked off by guards with halberds.

Trumpets and other instruments were being played, adding to the cacophony of sounds that drifted through the air. Caden spotted a few cloaked figures among the crowd, and he suspected they were some of his men. The people around them weren't affected by their appearance, and when one of them turned around, he saw why. They were wearing masks.

"Clever," he muttered to himself.

Bringing up the rear of the parade was a group of Runesmen decked out in armor. Commander Morin walked with them, and Caden was surprised to see that Lord D'Lance was present as well. He knew the man was wearing the pendant, despite the fact that he couldn't see it. If he thought it was valuable enough to sleep with, then he surely carried it on him now. Excitement welled within him. This was his opportunity to make amends for his failure. He just needed to wait until Bast and the others—

A commotion broke out near the guards blocking the main street when a group of draman cleared the area, forcing the city folk aside. The guards called for reinforcements, but before their help could arrive, the draman subdued them. The crowd surged away from the creatures, screaming about demons. Horns blared, and the Runesmen in the parade quickly made their way to the scene, but by then, a fight had broken out.

Soldiers and draman engaged in full battle, swords clanging. The city folk scattered in every direction, their screams and stampeding only adding to the chaos. Commander Morin joined the fray, swinging his blade with a fury that seemed impossible for a man his age. Caden watched it all from the roof, biding his time.

Lord D'Lance strode into the midst of the fighting and shouted for more soldiers. Caden couldn't wait any longer. He returned to the street and pushed his way through the throngs of fleeing people. All he needed to do was get near enough to steal the pendant, and then he would abscond with it back to his master.

He kept his sword sheathed as he neared the soldiers, dodging between the press of bodies to get closer. Lord D'Lance was only a few feet away and he was facing the other direction. Caden lunged forward, right hand reaching for the man's neck. His fingers grazed the chain at first, but he managed to grab hold of it and yanked it free. Lord D'Lance whirled around, and the two men locked gazes.

"You again. I'll have your head!"

Caden turned to flee and felt pain lance up his ribcage. He grunted and staggered, something wet slicking his skin. He knew without looking that he'd been stabbed. His vision grew hazy and he fell to the ground, the pendant skittering across the cobblestones.

13

Copper flapped his wings, lifting them higher. Mina's stomach churned uncomfortably as the dragon looped up and over the other beast, but she fought through the fear and fired her arrow, and then quickly wrapped her arms around Copper's neck, the bow dangling around her wrist as they flew upside down.

She couldn't see if the shot had struck the target, but once Copper leveled out, the giant brass dragon trumpeted at her and began to descend. Sitting dead center in the target he carried was her arrow. Mina whispered a prayer of thanks to Avera and sat up, looking for the next target.

There were three more, each one on the back of a silver dragon. They were gliding side by side, their scales shimmering brilliantly under the sun.

Are those the last targets?

Yes, Copper answered. *Silver dragons are quick, and they will be difficult to keep pace with. You'll need to strike as soon as we're within range.*

Mina prepared another arrow as Copper tried to catch up to them. The wind whipped her hair about wildly and she had to shield her eyes to keep them from drying out again. The nearest of the three dragons flew lazily, and once they were within range, the dragon zipped ahead, easily outdistancing Copper.

You weren't lying. They are fast!

Of course I wasn't lying. Dragons never lie.

Mina leaned forward as Copper flapped his wings faster, setting the bow in her lap. Copper's chest heaved with his breaths and his shoulders bumped her up and down.

Can you catch them? You seem to be struggling.

He growled in reply and flapped harder. Mina felt as if it took a while, but soon they were gaining on the dragon. It would occasionally slow down, then speed back up, and she realized that the creature was toying with them. It added fuel to the fire of her determination, and she readied her bow.

The other two are behind us, Copper said. *You might be able to get them both if you shoot fast enough.*

One target at a time.

Get ready. I'm going to close the distance, but as soon as she knows what I'm doing, she'll speed ahead.

I'm ready.

Copper shot forward suddenly, putting them within firing range. Mina took aim and fired, quickly pulling another arrow from the quiver. The projectile struck the very edge of the target, almost missing it.

That was close.

Too close, Copper replied. *I'm going to let the other two get ahead of me. Once we're behind them, you'll have to fire two arrows as fast as you can manage.*

At the same time?

No. That would be impossible.

Mina thought knocking two arrows back-to-back and hitting the targets would be impossible, but she had to try. Copper was too slow to match the silver dragons' speed, and if they lost this opportunity, she would never pass the test.

Hold on. It's going to get rough.

Mina pressed her legs into Copper's neck and grabbed two arrows from the quiver. She placed one in her lap and held onto the other, then braced herself. Copper lifted his wings up to catch the wind, and his bulk jerked backward. The two silver dragons continued past, and Mina lifted the bow and fired off the first arrow. It struck the target on the outer edge of the dragon to the left. Her fingers fumbled with the second arrow, and she almost dropped it. She struggled to knock it, her frustration adding to the hindrance. She got the arrow on the string and aimed, but the last target was just out of reach.

Hurry! Copper urged.

She swallowed hard and tilted the bow up a few inches and let the arrow fly. It soared through the air. A gust of wind blew it off mark and it missed the target, striking the wooden leg that supported it. Mina's heart sank into her stomach. She'd missed. The last two weeks had been for nothing. She bit her lip in anger and tried to keep her eyes from welling with tears. Copper descended slowly, but she lost focus on everything. Despair reared its ugly head.

They landed on the ground where the Enclave waited. Mina climbed down from Copper's back and walked over to stand before the elders. She kept her face as stoic as she could, but internally, she was screaming. She paused a few feet from the Enclave members and knelt.

Rise, the silver leader said.

Mina stood and waited to hear the crushing news.

You did well. The final target proved to be a challenge, but your arrow did strike it.

It did? Mina knew it had struck the leg, but she didn't think that counted. The dragon stared at her, and she realized she didn't use the proper title. *Apologies, Tiarna. I'm confused.*

Your task was to hit every target. You did so. What is there to be confused about?

I ... She cleared her throat. *I didn't think hitting the leg of the target counted.*

It is a technicality, but the Enclave has agreed to let it count. Prepare for your test with the blade.

Yes, Tiarna.

Mina turned around and walked back to Copper, a smile encompassing her face.

You did well, but two of those arrows came

close to missing. Keep your mind focused. If you let your guard down now, you won't make it.

I'm just happy that I didn't fail, she replied. *I thought for sure that last arrow wouldn't count as a strike.*

The Enclave is being generous, but do not expect the same leniency with the sword.

Mina drew her sword from the sheath and took a few practice swings.

How will they test my skill with a blade?

You will fight an opponent.

I have to fight a dragon?

No. You will fight Areg.

Areg? But he's ... she wanted to say dull, but she bit her tongue. *He's so small.*

Do not mistake his odd speech and size for a lack of intelligence. There is more to him than you know.

What do you mean?

I will tell you after your test. You need to remain focused.

The crowd of dragons closed in around them, forming a large makeshift ring. Areg stepped into the circle, wearing chainmail armor and carrying a sword. Mina wondered at the training Copper had given her. He'd trained her to use the bow on the ground, yet they tested her on dragon back. Now she was going to fight on the ground, but she'd trained in the air.

A hint of distrust washed over her, and she entertained the brief thought that he was trying to sabotage her. She looked at him and immediately pushed the thought away. Copper could have killed her long before now. And despite learning the bow on foot, she had managed to hit moving targets with his guidance. No, he wasn't trying to sabotage her.

How will one of us win? she asked.

You will battle until one of you has scored three hits. You should not seek to do mortal harm, but a little pain is acceptable. I'll let you know if the strike counts. The first to land three hits is the winner. Go and take your place.

Mina left Copper's side and walked to where Areg was.

"It me," he said.

"I hear you have some skill with these things." She shook the blade.

"Yes."

"Well, don't take it easy on me. I want a fair fight."

Areg smiled at her. "Me fight good."

"Let's see what you've got then."

He bowed to her, she mirrored the movement, and then he came at her with a ferocity she'd never seen before.

14

Caden scrambled ahead on all fours, grabbing the pendant and getting to his feet. Lord D'Lance was shouting incoherently behind him, but he ignored everything and ran along the street, turning down side alleys and zig-zagging his way through the city until he reached a random sewer grate.

His side throbbed painfully, and he spared a few seconds to look down. Whatever had struck him had cut right through his chainmail. Blood soaked his clothes, and judging by the amount of blood that trailed behind him, he knew the wound was deep. He knelt and pulled the grate aside, clenching his teeth against the pain. He just needed to reach the camp alive and one of the draman could get the pendant to their master.

Caden climbed down into the tunnel and walked blindly in the darkness, wandering in the direction he assumed would lead outside the city. As the minutes passed and his strength failed, he paused and leaned against the wall. He was losing too much blood.

Keep going.

His master's voice penetrated the veil of pain and weakness, energizing him. He forged ahead, keeping a quick but cautious pace. A rumbling sound reverberated through the tunnel, and the ground shuddered under his feet. What was going on above him?

The tunnel curved to the left, and daylight became visible. Caden exited the sewer and continued into the woods, but his vision was blurry and he struggled to put one foot in front of the other. He tripped and fell; the ground seeming to spin him round and round. He closed his eyes to ease the dizziness and the next thing he knew, he was on the back of a dragon, flying through the sky over The Long Sands.

Caden looked around, confused as to how he got there. Was he dead? Or if not, then why was he riding a dragon? He was also holding a bow, and he took aim and fired an arrow at another dragon. The projectile struck something on the creature's back, but he couldn't discern what it was. Suddenly, the scenery changed and he fell off the dragon, hurtling toward the ground.

Just as he was about to hit the ground, his eyes opened. He was lying on his back, staring up at the green canopy of the woods. The face of a draman looked down at him.

"You live," he said. "Good. The master would be furious if you died."

Caden touched his side. The wound was closed. He sat up to look and saw a long scar line, but otherwise, there was no sign that he'd been injured. His chainmail and sword had been removed and were lying nearby, but the pendant was missing.

"Where's the gemstone?"

The draman nudged the armor with his foot. Caden grabbed the edge of it and pulled it over, lifting it. The pendant fell to the ground. He breathed a sigh of relief and picked it.

"How did you close my wound?"

"It wasn't us. It was our master."

Thank you, Caden said, mentally pushing the words through the connection he felt with the dragon. She didn't respond, but he could sense her presence was still with him. He got to his feet and glanced around the camp. Bast and the others hadn't returned yet.

"Any word from the messengers?" he asked.

"No, sir. It's been silent."

That didn't sit well with Caden, especially considering how the events had unfolded before he escaped the city.

"If we don't get a report soon, send someone to investigate."

"As you command."

Caden slipped his chainmail back on and retrieved his sword sheath, strapping it around his waist. He wandered around the camp, killing time. He didn't want to leave while Bast was gone, but if he didn't return soon, Caden wouldn't have a choice. His master wanted to be free of her prison, and the gemstone in his possession was vital to achieving that freedom.

The smell of smoke reached his nostrils, and he

looked in the direction of Velbridge. The woods were too thick for him to see anything, but he was confident the scent wasn't from the campfires.

"Sir!" One of the draman flagged him down. "They've returned!"

Caden rushed across the camp. Bast and about twenty others marched through the trees. They were covered in blood and ash and looked exhausted. Bast met Caden's gaze and shook his head slightly.

"Let's speak in private," the draman said.

Caden walked with him until they were away from everyone else, and even then, Bast kept his voice low.

"We suffered heavy losses. Lord D'Lance brought out one of his dragons and it all went downhill from there."

"How many got out of the city?" Caden asked.

"I'm not sure. Those who returned with me are the only ones I can confirm."

Caden did his best not to let his expression reveal the alarm he felt. Out of four hundred men, only a handful returned to the camp.

"Where is the dragon now? Were you followed?"

"I think he lost control of it. It started burning the city. That's when we fled. I doubt he cared enough about us to give chase. His attention was diverted to a new crisis."

"Hopefully nobody was killed. The people have

no idea what kind of monster rules over them. The fact that he lost control of the dragon is a surprise, possibly a good one."

"Why is that?"

"It shows the creatures are fighting against his magic. If they can break free of his control, we could use that to our advantage."

"Our master is going to be upset when she learns that our forces are scattered and possibly dead."

"Maybe this will help." Caden held up the pendant.

Bast's eyes turned to slits. "Is that the stone she seeks?"

"Yes."

"How did you get it?"

Caden rubbed his chin, offering a slight grin. "I went into the city. Lord D'Lance was there, and I had the opportunity to take it, so I did."

"It will not please the master that you disobeyed her orders."

"She may already know. Either way, I had to redeem myself in her eyes. She gave me a task, and I needed to see it through to completion."

"I admire your determination, but you could have been killed."

"I nearly was," Caden said. "I took a deep cut to my side, but our master healed it. Here, you should take the gem to her. I'll stay here and work on regathering our men … if they are still alive out there."

"No. She will expect you to deliver it. You should take it to her now. Lord D'Lance will be looking for you, for all of us, and the further away you are from here, the better."

Caden looked across the camp at the other draman. He would feel guilty leaving them here, injured and alone.

"We were doing fine before you came, and we'll be fine without you," Bast said as if reading his mind. "Go."

"Very well. With any luck, I'll return with our master."

"It will be an honor to see her in the flesh."

Caden clapped a hand on Bast's shoulder and nodded, then walked to where he slept and gathered a few rations of food into a leather satchel. It would take a few hours to get to the mountain, and he was already feeling the pangs of hunger. He slung the bag over his shoulder and headed east, the pendant firmly in hand.

Lord D'Lance was going to pay dearly for his tyranny and slaughter.

15

Mina staggered backward under the fierceness of Areg's attack, almost tripping in her haste. The elf's diminutive size and unassuming nature deceived her, but now that she knew he was a trained warrior, she would not let her guard down. Mina brought her sword up to deflect his strikes, and their blades clanged loudly. The steel vibrated in her hand, sending an odd sensation along her arm.

I didn't train to fight an opponent this skilled!

You will not always be prepared for what you encounter in the world, Copper replied.

He always had an answer for everything she complained about, but it was never a resolution to her problem. She tried to remember what she'd heard Captain Eduard teach when Lord Klodian would visit the Runesman training grounds, but there was little she could recall. At the time, it hadn't seemed like information she would need to know.

She was so wrapped up in her thoughts that she didn't notice Areg was slowly pushing her into a corner until it was almost too late. The crowd of dragons watched intently, silently judging her progress. Areg outmatched her, but that didn't mean he was invincible. Mina dug her heels into the sand grabbed the hilt of her blade with both hands, driving the pointed end straight for Areg's chest.

The elf twirled aside, slapping her sword up high as he did so. She couldn't believe how graceful his movements were. They were in a battle, but he was so nimble that he seemed to dance more than anything. His feet capered over the sand, barely leaving an indentation at all. How was that possible?

Her thoughts shattered into a thousand pieces as stinging pain erupted along her wrist. Areg slapped the flat of his blade across her flesh, and he was already gone by the time she tried to jab at him.

That's one point for Areg.

Mina rubbed her wrist with to soothe the sting and watched the elf warily. He'd put some distance between them, and she took the brief respite to evaluate her lack of strategy. She had no doubt that she couldn't beat Areg, which meant that she would fail the test. Was this the Enclave's way of telling her that she wasn't fit to be a rider?

Focus, Copper's voice rumbled.

Sorry.

She shook her head as if that would dispel the thoughts from her mind and rolled her shoulders. Areg was staring at her, waiting.

I will do my best, she told herself.

Mina rushed toward Areg and swung her sword in an overhand chopping motion. She assumed she must look clumsy to everyone watching. Her movements were nowhere near as beautiful as Areg's. Yet again, he easily evaded her. As she passed him, unable to stop her momentum, he flashed her a grin and smacked the back of her knees with his sword.

Her legs buckled and gave way, sending her sprawling face-first into the sand. She got a mouthful of the gritty grains and spat repeatedly as she struggled to get back on her feet. Had this fight been in front of humans, there would be loud cheers and people heckling her. Instead, there was only silence as the dragons watched impassively.

I'm failing miserably, she complained.

Keep going. The tide can always change.

Mina wiped her mouth on the back of her hand, brushing the sand off. The ground trembled beneath her like it had earlier, and she looked around. Dragons glanced among themselves, and the smell of vanilla was overwhelming. She wished that their thoughts were available to her mind, as she could only wonder what they were saying to one another. She looked back at Areg, and he nodded at her.

"Fight," he said.

"I am."

He came at her like a flash of lightning, quick and terrifying. She barely brought her sword up in time to parry his strike, and the force ripped the hilt from her hand. The sword landed in the sand, and she threw herself to the ground to retrieve it. Areg was next to her immediately, his small foot landing a kick to her ribs. Despite his size, the blow was powerful and sent her rolling onto her back.

Mina could feel the ground still trembling, but now it was a constant vibration. She ignored Copper's announcement of the points as Areg placed his foot on her chest, preparing to land his final strike. She rolled away from him, latching onto the ankle of his other leg. Areg grunted as he fell on his back, temporarily stunned. She scrambled on all fours to her blade and snatched it out of the sand, then struck Areg's leg before he recovered.

Two to one in favor of Areg.

At least I finally hit him, but he only needs one more point. It's impossible for me to win.

Keep going, Copper repeated.

Mina got to her feet, chest heaving. Sweat was rolling down her arms and legs, and sand clung to her flesh. This type of fighting was harder than she thought. Areg stalked around her like a predator, and she turned with him, keeping her eyes locked on his. Copper was right, there *was* more to him than she knew.

As if reading each other's minds, they lunged toward one another at the same time. Their blades clashed as they fought in close proximity, and for a fleeting moment, Mina thought she might hold her own against Areg.

The elf dropped to his knees and jabbed his sword upward, hitting her in the stomach with the tip. Her armor kept the sword from impaling her, but pain still flared through her abdomen at the strike. Mina clenched her jaw against the pain and stumbled backward.

Three to one in favor of Areg, Copper said.

I lost, Mina mentally gasped.

Yes, but you did well. Areg is a skilled warrior, and you lasted longer than I expected.

Mina found that difficult to believe, but it eased the sting of her loss until she realized that she'd failed the test. The Enclave would deny her request to hold off the war, and humanity would burn under their wrath.

You did well, the silver dragon's voice entered her mind.

I lost. How is that doing well?

Your small amount of training has proven that you do have what it takes to be a warrior. You could never have defeated Areg, even if you had trained for years rather than weeks.

Then why did you put me against him?

We have our reasons, the dragon vaguely replied.

Since I failed, will you go to war?

You might have lost, but you did not fail. We will not go to war against the humans.

Mina had never felt more relief in her entire life.

Thank you for trusting me. I will do whatever I must to stop Lord D'Lance.

Good. You must kill him, else he will never stop.

I will do what must be done, Mina said. She didn't agree to kill him, but if that's what needed to be done when the time came, then she would do it. She sheathed her blade and knelt, embracing Areg in a hug.

"Where did you learn to fight like that?" she asked.

"Story long."

Before she could say anything, there was an unearthly roar that hurt her ears. She clasped her hands over them and snapped her gaze to Copper.

What was that?

One of the scouts, he replied. *We're under attack.*

From who?

Sand wyrms.

16

Caden found the climb up the mountain less arduous than the first time, but it still proved to be an exhausting task. The sky was clear, a vibrant blue, and the sun beat down directly on him. Sweat seemed to come from his every pore, but unlike the first journey, he stopped periodically to rest and eat the provisions he'd brought.

As he topped the ridge where the abandoned temple's entrance was, he had a sense of foreboding. Now that he knew the voice that had called to him belonged to a dragon, he was unsure about many things. Still, he reminded himself that she had brought him back from death, healed him, and given him charge over her army of draman.

Caden inhaled a deep breath to calm his nerves and entered the cave. The darkness was thick, but he remembered there should be light ahead. When he encountered the glowing moss, he knew that he was getting close. His steps were sure, despite the thundering pace of his heart. The tunnel brought him into the abandoned temple, and the glowing eyes of his master peered at him from the shadows. He swallowed hard and drew as close to her as he dared.

Caden, my devoted servant. I sense something different about you.

"I'm not sure what you mean," he replied.

There is something keeping your thoughts from me. You haven't betrayed me, have you?

"No, of course not. I owe you my life. I could never forsake my oath."

Good, she hissed. *Why have you come here?*

Caden retrieved the pendant from his satchel and held it up for her to see. The dragon growled, low and dangerous.

That is why you feel distant. That cursed stone is the bane of my existence. You must destroy it for me.

"Gladly," Caden said.

He dropped the pendant to the ground and drew his sword, then struck the portion holding the stone with all his might. He inspected his work, but the stone wasn't even scratched.

Your enthusiasm is commendable, but normal weapons cannot destroy the stone.

"Then how?"

You must take it to where it was created and use words of power to unravel its magic.

"I am not a sorcerer, so I do not know what words would be used. Should I seek one out?"

No. I will teach you the words needed. They do not need to come from a sorcerer, they only need to be spoken.

"Where do I need to take the stone?"

At the pinnacle of the mountain. Lord D'Lance

crafted his dark magic there and tricked me, imprisoning me and stealing my eggs. You will go there and speak the words I teach you. When the gemstone is broken, I shall be free.

Caden put the pendant back into the satchel and sheathed his blade. The air was thin at this altitude, and he wondered if he had the fortitude to make it further up. He would try regardless, because he had given his word to her.

The wind is strong up there, so take your steps prudently. If you fall, you will perish.

"I will heed caution. If I die before you are free, then I have failed in my duties."

Good. Remember these words: Cealaigh an draíocht seo agus oscail an méid atá curtha faoi ghlas. When you reach the top, speak them and it will undo the dark magic binding me here. Repeat them.

Caden stumbled over them a few times, but on the sixth try he spoke them perfectly.

Now go. I want to be free of this place before the sun sets.

He offered a slight bow and left, making his way back out to the ledge. His gaze roamed the upper portion of the mountain. Rocks jutted up everywhere, enormous and jagged, and the peak seemed so far away.

"I can do this," he muttered to himself.

He started making his way up, picking the route

carefully. The higher he climbed, the more powerful the wind whipped. The temperature dropped as well, and the sun did little to warm him. Caden was making good progress before he tripped. A small, flat rock shifted under his weight and sent him careening backward. His arms rotated in circles as he fell, but there was nothing for him to grab ahold of, and he tumbled for twenty feet until he roughly came to a stop, wedged between two boulders.

His mind hadn't fully comprehended what had happened, and he sat there unmoving for a long while. Pain lanced through his chest with every breath, and he knew that something was broken, likely a few ribs. He tried to communicate with his master, but then he recalled what she'd said about the stone blocking his thoughts.

Caden refused to die, at least not here, and he forced himself to get up. His right side was the source of his pain, and he gingerly pressed a hand onto his ribcage. He sucked in a sharp breath and used his other hand to steady himself as he grew lightheaded. Once the weakness passed, he continued his ascent.

It took him a long time to reach the area where he'd fallen, and even longer to find a safe path ahead. The mountain was a veritable death trap, and he cursed Lord D'Lance in his thoughts with every setback. The man had done well to ensure no one would be foolish enough to seek the place where he'd created his spell. Perhaps Caden was foolish, or just brazenly insane, but he forced himself to continue the trek.

The peak was only a few hundred feet away now. He wasn't sure if it was the lack of oxygen or his imagination, but he thought he could see something glowing. It was a translucent pale shade of blue, and whatever it was, it cast its light around the entire mountaintop.

"I'm losing my mind," Caden said, unsure exactly why he was talking to himself. He laughed at the thought, causing his ribs to flare with agony, but the pain brought a semblance of clarity. He was almost there, and while he wasn't truly losing his sanity, he was being affected by the thinness of the air.

Caden's movements became sluggish, and his vision was blurred. He jostled his side, and the pain brought his focus back, but only for a short time. Eventually, even that did nothing to help him keep his wits. At one point, it startled him to realize that he was sitting on a rock and hadn't been walking at all.

His satchel was on the ground at his feet, open. The rations were gone, and his canteen was empty. When had he partaken of them? His mind was muddled. He spotted the pendant on the ground and picked it up, standing on unsteady legs. There was a reason he had this, a reason he'd come up here to begin with. What was it?

Then he remembered, though the memory was foggy. He needed to take it to the top of the mountain … for some reason or other. He continued up the steep slope, finally reaching the base of the plateau where the glowing light was coming from.

Caden staggered up the last few feet and found a pool of water. It bubbled, wisps of steam rising from its surface.

It was a hot spring. The water looked warm and inviting. He'd made it, so he deserved a break, didn't he? He tried to step closer, but the pale blue light turned out to be a magical barrier, keeping him from going any further.

Now what was he supposed to do?

17

The host of dragons around Mina and Areg took to the air, creating a mini sandstorm in their wake. Mina buried her face into the crook of her arm and waited until she could see, then ran to Copper.

You said sand wyrms aren't smart enough to band together.

They're not.

Then why are they attacking?

I'm not sure, but I suspect it has something to do with Lord D'Lance. Get on my back. It's not safe being on the ground.

She climbed up onto his back and looked at Areg.

Will he be safe underground?

Yes, but I doubt he'll willingly go down there.

Mina motioned to him. "Come on!"

The elf rushed over to them and easily clambered up Copper to sit behind her. He wrapped his small arms around her and held on tightly. Copper launched into the air and ascended high above the ground. Mina scoured the landscape and spotted the approaching sand wyrms. The ground heaved upward as they tunneled through the sand, heading for the dragon cave.

There are so many of them.

Something has driven them here, Copper replied. *There is nothing natural about this.*

The other dragons were circling in the air, roaring challenges at the wyrms. Mina was worried. If Lord D'Lance was controlling the creatures, what was he trying to accomplish?

He probably knows we're aware of his scheme.

How would he be controlling them, though?

Magic. The same kind he's using to force bonds with.

One of the wyrms broke free of the ground, rising into the air like a monolith. Its thick flesh rippled, and Mina scowled in disgust. The dragons attacked it with fury, clawing and biting at its exposed body. It screeched in pain, and two more wyrms ascended from the sand nearby.

Are there enough dragons to drive them back?

Yes.

There was something about the way he answered that made Mina think he wasn't entirely confident. She could smell a hint of lavender. Copper was afraid.

How can I help? she asked.

You can't. They're too strong for you to injure. Driving a sword into one would be useless, and getting that close would get you killed. We will stay in the air and wait for them to flee.

As more wyrms continued to breach the sand, Mina feared that Copper was wrong about the strength of the dragons' numbers. They hadn't killed one yet, and none of the wyrms were trying to escape the wrath of tooth and talon.

How can Lord D'Lance be controlling them from so far away?

Copper hummed in thought. *He may be out here somewhere, though I doubt it.*

One of the wyrms began bleating, but it didn't seem to be a cry of pain. Mina watched it, wondering what it was doing. The other wyrms joined it, producing a chorus of deep rumbling cries.

Something is coming.

More wyrms?

Copper didn't answer, but a moment later, the ground erupted as a wyrm twice the size of the others broke free. Black spines lined its body, and its maw was full of razor-sharp teeth. It roared like a dragon, its eyeless face swishing back and forth as if searching for an enemy to battle.

"Wyrm king!" Areg shouted from behind her.

"What's that?"

It's trouble, Copper answered. *They are harder to kill than the others. The heart is its only weak spot, and it's encased in a thick layer of bone and muscle and buried too deep to be reached by dragon claws.*

Then how do you strike its heart?

It must be done from the inside.

You don't mean ...

Yes, Copper confirmed. *The one to kill it must be swallowed.*

That's certain death!

For some, yes. But there are a rare few who have survived to tell the tale.

Have you?

Copper chortled. *No, but Areg has.*

Mina twisted awkwardly to look back at the elf.

"You've killed one of those?"

He grinned. "Me kill two."

Two. Areg had killed two wyrm kings. He was an expert swordsman and a phenomenal shot with the bow. She couldn't help but wonder who the little elf truly was.

"Take close," he said, a gleam in his eyes. He patted the hilt of his sword.

I'm going to fly over the wyrm so Areg can deal with the beast.

Mina slid her fingers under Copper's scales and gripped them tightly. Copper turned in the direction of the wyrm king and sped straight for it. A host of dragons had swarmed the creature, and Mina gasped in horror as the spines on the wyrm's body shot free, impaling several of the dragons. Their broken bodies fell from the sky.

Stay low, Copper advised.

Mina leaned forward, practically laying on his neck. The wyrm roared as they flew over it, and despite their altitude, Mina could feel the warmth of its breath on her skin. Areg released her and she saw him leap off Copper's back from her peripheral. She winced as the elf disappeared into the mouth of the wyrm.

I hope he survives.

It will take more than a sand wyrm to kill him.

Copper continued, wheeling around and ascending higher into the sky. Mina looked from wyrm to wyrm. The dragons had numbers on their side, but they were smaller in size than the bulky wyrms.

You said you would tell me about Areg after my tests. Who is he? How is he so good with weapons?

Areg is an elf, and they have a natural gift when it comes to agility and speed, but that is not what makes him different. He was once a rider, bonded to a dragon like you.

That took Mina by surprise. She struggled to wrap her mind around the information.

You said he was a rider. He's not now?

No. Sadly, his bonded passed away many years ago. He's remained with us ever since, pledging his life to help us however possible.

Why does he talk so odd?

Areg aided in the battle against Maël, and he was struck by a spell that damaged his mind. He's spoken that way ever since, but otherwise, he is the same as he was back then. I have never known a braver elf than Areg.

That explains a lot, Mina said. *When you said I was the first rider in a thousand years, I thought that meant there weren't any other riders alive.*

Areg is the only one.

Mina didn't understand why the elf chose to live with the dragons instead of his own people, but she guessed he had his reasons. Her attention returned to the wyrms and the unfolding battle. The situation looked grim. More dragons had fallen, and no wyrms were dead. She saw the silver dragon who led the Enclave leading a group toward the wyrm king.

Looks like she's got a plan.

Copper swiveled his head and Mina felt him tense.

She's going to get herself killed. I need to stop her.

I go where you go, Mina replied.

She could sense his hesitation through the scale. That was a new experience.

Go, she urged. *We must protect her.*

Copper dived toward the wyrm king, roaring thunderously. Mina was afraid and excited all at the same time, and she held on to Copper as firmly as she could. The wyrm king released more spines, and one of them flew directly at Copper. He swerved sharply to avoid it, and Mina's eyes widened as his scales slipped free of her sweaty hands.

She fell off his back and tumbled through the air.

18

Caden stared at the flickering blue barrier and considered his options. The reason he brought the stone up here still eluded him, so it likely wasn't too important. Was it something he wanted to do, or someone else? The answer hovered at the edge of his mind, but it was clouded with uncertainty.

He looked back the way he'd come and considered going back down, but he couldn't find a reason to do that, either. It was as if he were in a battle of tug-of-war, the two opposing thoughts vying for control of his mind, and the pressure made him tired. Caden wanted nothing more than to rest, but a strange force wouldn't let him.

"Please," he begged. "I can't do it."

The force increased, and he dropped to his knees, the pain in his ribs causing him to cry out in agony. The two forces continued to clash in his mind, and one gained control.

Touch the gemstone to the barrier.

The voice was familiar. It was … his master? Yes, that seemed right. He lifted his hand and pressed the pendant to the barrier. At first, the blue light intensified, blinding him. A sizzling noise filled his ears, and the barrier blinked out of existence. Warmth washed over him, driving back the chill in his bones. He crawled forward and reached the bubbling pool. The water stank of rotten eggs, making him gag.

Get in the water. That is the source of the magic.

He didn't want to, but he would obey her regardless. Rising to his feet, he hesitantly stepped into the pool. The water was blue, a much different shade from the barrier. Its color was deceiving, though, given its smell. The temperature was hot, uncomfortably so, but he pressed on at the urging of his master.

Go to the center. It will be the deepest spot.

The water grew too deep for him to reach the bottom, and it forced him to swim. He reached the middle and treaded the water to keep his head from going under.

Now speak the words I told you.

Caden tried to remember them, but the fog in his mind hadn't fully lifted yet. His muscles ached, and his ribs burned fiercely. It was all he could do to keep from sinking, and when he went under, he sunk like a sack of rocks. Water flooded into his mouth and he panicked. His feet touched something solid, and he kicked off of it, splashing above the water's surface. He coughed and sputtered, fighting to stay afloat.

Say the words!

He was trying not to drown, and his master wanted him to speak some magical words he could barely recall. Fear flooded him. He was going to fail. He was going to *die*. Despite his brush with death on the plains, Caden was still afraid of the unknown.

Say them!

Caden went under the water again, but this time he was prepared. He held his breath and touched the bottom, springing himself above the pool's surface again. The words came to him then, and he shouted them as loudly as he could.

"Cealaigh an draíocht seo agus oscail an méid atá curtha faoi ghlas!"

He fell beneath the waer, and the pendant in his hand shivered. The gemstone shattered, and an invisible force escaped from it, sending ripples through the water. The fragments of the stone fell free of the pendant and drifted down to the bottom of the pool. Before he could try to get out of the water, it churned in a circular motion, quickly becoming a maelstrom.

The current swept Caden along, spinning him around and around. He tried to grab onto the edge of the pool, but his hands kept slipping off the slick surface. The maelstrom spun faster and suddenly shot up into the air. Caden was pushed aside, and he struck the ground with a grunt and laid on his back, watching the geyser of water rise into the sky, pain shooting through his chest.

As it came back down, it spread out and landed everywhere but in the pool, disappearing into the soil or rolling down the sides of the mountain. Caden couldn't believe he'd succeeded. The entire situation felt unreal, more like a dream than anything.

My shackles are free!

His master's voice was filled with emotion, a mix of excitement and relief tinged with anger. The ground under his feet trembled, reminding him of being in the sewers under Velbridge. The pain in his ribs subsided, and a wave of strength invigorated him. He sat up and looked around, wondering where the tremors were coming from.

You have kept your oath and freed me. I am most pleased with you, and you shall be my right hand among my forces. I shall lead my brethren to war, and you shall lead my draman.

"I am honored!" Caden shouted, his words echoing into the sky. "You saved me from death, and I shall serve you for the rest of my days!"

His master's pleasure pulsed through him, filling his veins with fire. He could also feel her rage boiling under the surface of all of her other emotions, kept in check … for now. Lord D'Lance had made a grave mistake by trapping her in the mountain.

The tremors in the ground strengthened, and in the distance, one peak crumbled, spilling boulders and dirt down the slopes below. Caden hurried to the edge of the plateau and looked down. Avalanches of stone tumbled down the mountain, obliterating the path he'd taken. It seemed as if the entire mountain was going to split in two. He needed to get to safety, but there was no way he could climb down without being crushed.

Stay where you are, his master said. *I will get you.*

Far below, an explosion rocked the ground, and debris scattered from the ridge where the temple was. A massive form as dark as the night sky came forth, swatting the boulders aside as if they were nothing more than small bugs. She turned and winged her way toward him, and Caden was overcome with fear and awe.

He fell to his knees in reverence but kept his eyes locked on her beauty. Her scales were black as ebony, her wings easily twice the size of Lord D'Lance's castle grounds. She was massive in every regard. She opened her mouth and breathed fire, huge gouts of orange flames ripping through the sky. Even from this distance, he could feel the heat of them.

She landed on the peak where the pool of water had been, and she raked the ground with her claws, tearing the rock apart and flinging it away. When she finished, he couldn't tell that anything had been there at all. She roared, the sound louder than anything he'd ever heard before. He clapped his hands over his ears. The dragon narrowed her gaze on him and snaked her head forward, emerald eyes blazing as hot as her flames.

Now this world is going to burn.

19

Mina screamed in terror.

Above her, Copper weaved back and forth, dodging the black spines. A hundred thoughts passed through her mind, but mainly she feared that Copper didn't know she'd fallen off of his back. She maneuvered herself face-down toward the ground and immediately regretted it. Seeing the desert landscape speeding toward her was like looking death straight in the face.

Before she could prepare for her untimely demise, a massive claw grabbed ahold of her, breaking her freefall. Her body whipped harshly to a stop, but she was alive. She looked up to see the large brass dragon from her test.

Thank you. She pushed the words through the scale, but the dragon didn't respond. He ascended higher and Mina saw that the dragons were falling back, retreating from the wyrms. Had they lost?

Dragons don't give up that easily, Copper said. *We're regrouping.*

He swooped in below her, matching the brass dragon's pace. The dragon released her, and she fell a few feet down onto Copper's back.

I thought I was going to die.

You're lucky that Gavar saw you fall. He was the only one close enough to catch you.

Mina watched Gavar as he flew toward the horde of dragons gathering near one of the wyrms. She expressed her gratitude again through the scale, but she didn't know if he heard her.

I'm glad he helped me. I don't think I've proven myself enough yet, and I want to live long enough to do so.

If Gavar didn't think you were worthy of being a rider, he wouldn't have saved you.

The group of dragons were circling above the wyrm, staying high enough that it couldn't reach them. That didn't stop it from trying, and it screeched in frustration.

What are they planning?

We've lost too many of our brethren to divide ourselves, so we're going to attack them one at a time, Copper replied. *Once Areg kills the wyrm king, the others should flee, regardless of the magic being used on them.*

I hope you're right.

Copper joined the other dragons, and together they descended and began breathing fire on the wyrm. The heat washed over Mina, heavy and thick like a weighted blanket, forcing her to shield her face in the crook of her arm. Just when she thought it would become too much to bear, Copper broke away and the heat subsided.

Are you all right?

The heat is intense, but I'm fine.

The wyrm's cries of pain drowned out everything else, and Mina shuddered at the sound. Dragons swarmed the beast a second time, their fiery breath blistering and burning the wyrm's flesh, and the third attack silenced its cries forever.

Mina didn't know which was worse, the heat or the stench. With the first wyrm dead, the dragons turned their attention to the next one and began attacking it the same way. Mina was awed by the power of the dragons. Working together, they seemed like an unstoppable force. This wyrm fell quicker than the first one, and as they flew toward the third, a shrill keen came from the wyrm king.

The giant monster's body went limp, and it crashed down onto the sand, sending shock waves rolling across the desert. Mina couldn't believe that Areg had been successful. If what Areg told her was true, then he had now killed three wyrm kings. It seemed to her an impossible feat, something she could never accomplish.

The rest of the wyrms immediately began burrowing back into the sand, fleeing the area. It relieved Mina to see them go. Copper joined the silver Enclave leader and they landed near the body of the wyrm king. Mina had thought the creature massive before, but as she stood on the ground next to it, she felt like a grain of sand next to a mountain.

Are you sure it's dead? she asked.

As if in reply, a slit appeared on the beast's side and the flesh ripped open. Areg staggered out, wiping blood and entrails from his face and casting the gruesomeness to the ground. The dragons roared, a cry of victory rising to the heavens.

"It me," Areg said.

Mina laughed. She felt as if it had been an eternity since the last time she'd done so, and it eased the stress from her. The silver Enclave leader joined them, and she fixed her gaze on Mina.

This attack on our home cannot go unpunished.

You said you weren't going to war.

And I will keep my word, but I am going to send a small force of dragons to harass Lord D'Lance. They will travel with you and your bonded as protectors, but their first duty is to exact revenge for this affront.

I thought you wanted me to kill him?

The smell of lemon and clove hit Mina's nostrils.

I do, but I doubt that Lord D'Lance will be an easy target. My hope is that when my brethren are attacking his castle, he'll put himself in the open where you can strike. And if you die, then we will have our war.

I understand, Tiarna.

Mina desperately hoped that she could do what was needed to avoid a war, but her confidence was shaken. If Lord D'Lance could control beasts as large and powerful as the sand wyrms, what else was he capable of?

We will feast tonight, and in the morning, you

shall deliver our wrath to that wretched man.

Yes, Tiarna.

—

By the time Mina tiredly stumbled into her chamber to get some sleep, it was late into the night. She removed her armor and flopped onto her bed. The sounds of dragons still celebrating their victory over the sand wyrms echoed faintly off the walls, but her exhaustion ensured that wasn't a problem, and she fell into the darkness of sleep.

When she awoke, the first thing she noticed was the soreness in her muscles. A groan escaped her lips as she sat up and looked around. Her armor was on the manakin again, and she suspected it was Areg who had placed it there.

I wondered if you would sleep all day, Copper said.

How late is it?

It's morning, but the sun has been up for a few hours now.

Mina rolled her eyes and got out of bed. She'd eaten so much the night before that she wasn't hungry for breakfast. She donned her armor and put her boots on, then headed into Copper's room. Despite the oddity of living with dragons in an underground cave for the last few weeks, she was going to miss the place.

I get to keep the armor and sword, right?

Yes, it is a gift from the Enclave.

I suppose I'm ready to leave if you are.

There is one more thing I must give you.

What is it?

You asked my name, and I told you that I would give it to you when you earned my trust.

Mina sucked in a breath. The silence seemed to stretch unendingly until he finally spoke.

My name is Gedrith.

I'm honored that you have come to trust me, Mina said, full of emotion.

And I am honored that we are bonded, Copper, now Gedrith, replied.

They stood quietly for a moment, and then Mina rushed forward and wrapped her arms around his leg, hugging it tightly. She had once only known hatred for dragons, and now she called one friend.

So am I, Gedrith. So am I.

The two of them went to see the Enclave to wish them farewell, and then they took to the air, heading for the Dracan Dominion. Mina was soaring over the clouds, literally and figuratively. She wanted nothing more than to see Caden, to tell him of everything that had happened to her since he'd left. She just needed to survive her encounter with Lord D'Lance, which didn't seem likely.

You will not die at his hands.

Why are you so sure?

I'm not. But if you do, I'll scorch him from

existence in vengeance.

Mina smiled. Having a dragon at her back was all she needed. Gedrith was right. She would survive.

And then she would be free.

THE END OF BOOK THREE

ABOUT THE AUTHOR

Richard Fierce is a fantasy and space opera author. He's been writing since childhood, but began publishing in 2007. Since then, he's written multiple novels and short stories.

In 2000, Richard won Poet of the Year for his poem *The Darkness*. He's also one of the creative brains behind the Allatoona Book Festival, a literary event in Acworth, Georgia.

A recovering retail worker, he now works in the tech industry when he's not busy writing.

He's married and has three step-daughters (pray for him), a grandson, three dogs (huskies!), four cats, and two ferrets. He basically has a zoo.

His love affair with fantasy was born in high school when a friend's mother gave him a copy of *Dragons of Spring Dawning* by Margaret Weis and Tracy Hickman.

www.ingramcontent.com/pod-product-compliance
Lightning Source LLC
Chambersburg PA
CBHW021248200726
48288CB00015B/3046